# Life After War

# Also by Monty R. Garner

*Buckshot*

# Life After War

## Sawyer McCade
### Book 1

## Monty R. Garner

**WOLFPACK**
**PUBLISHING**
— EST 2013 —

**Life After War**
Paperback Edition
Copyright © 2025 (As Revised) by Monty R. Garner

Wolfpack Publishing
1707 E. Diana Street
Tampa, FL 33610

www.wolfpackpublishing.com

Paperback ISBN 979-8-89567-250-1
Ebook ISBN 979-8-89567-249-5

# Life After War

# Chapter One

*They're dead! They are all dead!*

Those were the young soldier's thoughts as he woke up and looked around at the desolation where he lay. His eyes wouldn't focus completely, and he saw the corpses of soldiers lying on the ground around him through the blurry haze that was the result of his injuries. He lay in the shallow ditch trying to comprehend what had happened through the confusion that bewildered his brain. He couldn't think straight for the pain at the back of his skull.

*What's wrong with my head? Did I get shot or clubbed from behind?*

With some difficulty he rolled onto his side, put his hand to the back of his head, and felt the goose egg there that seemed to be caked with blood.

The constant pain had a crippling effect on him; he closed his eyes to block out the throb and discomfort. A few moments later, the pounding ache began to subside and he remembered something. His orders from yesterday. He, along with two other soldiers, had been

1

ordered to spy on the small Union encampment located twenty-two miles southwest of Chalks Bluff, Arkansas. They'd snuck in after midnight and gotten close enough to the campsite to see the few scattered tents and the remains of campfires, which were nothing more than smoldering coals. And that was all he could recall.

The number one objective now was to see if he had been shot or had any other injuries besides the lump on the back of his head. He moved his hand slowly along his arms, legs, and abdomen in search of a bullet wound or broken bone. Although his clothes were damp, he quickly dispelled the notion that it was blood and instead most likely just early-morning dew. The pain at the back of his head intensified again as he felt it and when he checked his fingers, they were covered with blood. He surmised that someone had probably hit him with the butt of a rifle and left him for dead. He had lain there since last night and couldn't remember anything about the skirmish that had caused so many soldiers to lose their lives.

He had to think about what to do and where he could go until he found help. His detachment had been on the move when he left yesterday, and if they had been involved in the skirmish, he would have to find them. He rested on his back and looked up at the heavens to see buzzards high in the sky, circling the encampment. He was a trained scout and tracker who relied on his senses for protection. He knew to listen to the sounds around him. He heard birds chirping—that meant no one but him was there, or the birds would have flown off. He raised his head enough to see the field occupied by Union tents and dead Bluecoats. Two rabbits scurried for food around each campfire picking up scraps of food from the ground, which gave him additional confidence that he was alone.

The distant sound of gunfire got his attention and he tried to determine which direction it came from. Based on the echo of the sound, it must have been coming from more than a mile away, southwest of his location. It was time that he moved to find cover in case the Bluecoats came back toward the camp. He needed his rifle, but where was it? Frantically, the soldier moved to the side of the ditch and felt for his rifle, but to no avail. It wasn't there. Anxiety, fright and uncertainty caused him to lie still, take deep breaths and think. He was hurt, with no gun or means to protect himself. What a predicament to be in. With his eyes closed to ease the pain in the back of his head, his next task was to find a weapon and get to a safe location that could be defended in case the Union soldiers came back.

# Chapter Two

In 1863, Sawyer McCade joined the Confederate army at the age of twenty-two, along with his two best friends, Matt Rural and Tony Stevens, even though their folks were sympathetic to the Union and against slavery. He grew up in Kansas, and he and his two buddies all lived on adjoining farms. They had learned to work hard and did everything together, like hunting, fishing or just playing when they weren't working.

In the first month of their service, the three young men were assigned under the command of Brigadier General John S. Marmaduke who was stationed in southern Missouri with a force of five thousand men. From previous engagements with the Union, his troops were short of weapons, ammunition, and food. The general split his resources into two detachments with the plan to overtake the Union garrison at Cape Girardeau, Missouri. Sawyer, along with his friends, was assigned to advance on the town with Colonel George W. Carter while the rest of the troops went to another location to set a trap for the retreating Union soldiers.

Colonel Carter and his men got bogged down in the swamps on the way to Cape Girardeau, and both Matt and Tony were killed by snipers when they finally exited the swamps. Sawyer was devastated by what he saw and the loss of his friends. He struggled to stay engaged with the rest of the troops and when they finally reached Cape Girardeau, the Union troops had already left. He became enraged with sadness, anger and the realization that he could also be killed. He took on a whole new attitude and fought with a determination for survival that didn't go unnoticed by his superiors. He was assigned to serve under a guerrilla leader, Captain William Quantrill.

Quantrill's men trained Sawyer to be a reconnaissance scout to spy on the opposing forces. Along with that training, he was taught how to kill with not only weapons but also with his hands. Learning how to spy on the opposing forces had come easy to the young man, and when his superiors saw the stringent work ethic and strong leadership he imposed on his fellow recruits, they gave him more responsibility. In July of 1864, he was reassigned to Brigadier General M. Jeff Thompson, Commander for the Army of the Northern Sub-District of Arkansas, as sergeant and lead scout. His job was to spy on Union camps and convey his findings back to his superiors so they could develop a plan of attack. He had been taught to infiltrate the enemy, kill or inflict as much pain as possible, and not have a conscience about taking another human life during war. War is a cruel and disheartening episode in a young man's life when he has to become a killing machine to survive.

# Chapter Three

Sawyer pulled himself up enough so he could lean on his elbows and survey his surroundings the best he could. To his left ran a split-rail fence, and Confederate soldiers lay dead on the ground along one side. A few were slumped over the rails and a couple had even broken the fence when they'd fallen on it.

To his right were the remains of the Union encampment where men in blue uniforms lay dead in the field where they had their tents and campfires situated. Some of the tents were on the ground where soldiers had fallen on them when they were shot. A few tents that were still standing had corpses nearby and no one seemed to be moving, from what he could see, but he was still cautious. One thing he had learned during his fighting days was not to take things for granted and make himself a target.

Gunshots could still be heard from the south, but it seemed like the sounds were farther away now. The corpses in the battlefield must be giving off an odor since it looked like more buzzards were circling in the sky. As soon as it got hot and the bodies decomposed, he would be able to smell the stench of rotted flesh.

By pulling himself forward with his arms, he crawled down the shallow ditch on his stomach. When he came to the first dead soldier obstructing his way by lying crossways across the ditch, he pulled himself over the corpse and kept going. The edge of the woods was in front of him and that was where he would take cover until he decided what to do next.

A few feet to the right of the ditch was a Yankee officer lying face down in the grass, still holding onto his pistol. Sawyer thought about his chances of exiting the ditch to retrieve the weapon without getting shot. He needed a gun. The rifle he had been using was a single shot, and the Colt Dragoon Revolver the officer had could shoot six times before reloading, so he decided to take his chances and go after the pistol. He lay still and listened to the sounds around him to make sure no one was moving among the trees. He could hear birds chirping and leaves rustling in the wind. Like a scared lizard, he scurried on his belly out of the ditch and over to the dead officer and pried the man's stiff fingers from the gun handle.

Upon examination, the cylinders were empty so he needed to find lead and powder to arm the weapon. Using all his strength, he turned the man over and removed the Army-issued holster from around the Union soldier's waist. The officer had a leather bag draped over his neck and shoulder. Inside the bag, he found firing caps, lead, wadding, and a powder flask. A quick search of the officer's pockets revealed nothing else that he could use except twenty-four dollars in Union Greenbacks.

Sawyer rolled back into the ditch and loaded the gun with caps, black powder, and lead. It was a slow process, but he needed his weapon ready to fire in case there was trouble. When the gun was loaded, he slung his scabbard over his shoulder and continued to crawl toward the line of trees. The ditch got deeper as it entered the woods. There was now more than enough cover, so he climbed out of the trench and stood on weak legs to look around.

Even though he had first thought there were dozens of dead men, he now saw probably fewer than thirty bodies. He had to make sure that no Yankee soldiers were alive and waiting to shoot him if he happened to expose himself. The ditch he'd been in ran north and south through what seemed like a couple of acres of grass field. The trees where he stood were on the south side of the field, which put the tents to his north. Staying just inside the tree line, he crept on his stomach west until he was directly south of the tents. He crawled to the very edge of the field and watched the tents since he now had a different view. He couldn't see any movement and decided to advance on foot, crouched over with the pistol in his hand, ready to shoot.

Since only seven tents still stood, he went from one to another without finding anyone alive. The tents that were collapsed on the ground didn't pose a threat to him since most of those had a dead soldier weighing them down. Even though he now had a weapon and some ammunition, he searched the dead Union soldiers for more lead and gunpowder for his gun. Another of the soldiers also had a pistol, so he took it and loaded its cylinder. He felt much better now that he had two fully loaded guns and could shoot twelve shots before reloading. He rifled through a total of nine Union corpses and came away with two guns, an abundance of powder and lead, and thirty-eight dollars in Greenbacks, which was more money than he had ever had in his life.

It was time to retreat and find his company. He hoped they were still where he had left them yesterday, but the continued sound of gunfire off in the distance made him wonder if they had moved or retreated farther to the south.

# Chapter Four

With two loaded guns secured in holsters around his waist, Sawyer started out to find his way back to his company of fellow soldiers. As he crossed over the split-rail fence where dead soldiers lay, he recognized one of the other spies who had come with him the night before among the bodies. He stopped long enough to pick up the man's weather-ridden flop hat and put it on his own head for protection from the spring sun. He and the rest of his fellow soldiers had welcomed the April sunshine of 1865 when their winter clothes were almost nonexistent and had a hard time keeping out the cold winter. The warm spring was comforting since they had endured the cold with few provisions that winter.

Now he wore a battered, dirty, brown linen shirt that he had taken off a dead civilian in Missouri and a pair of butternut-colored britches that had rips in both knees. All his clothes were so worn and thin that they tore easily when snagged on a branch. The Army-issued brogan boots leaked water, and the leather soles had holes in them. Like many other soldiers, he had put a small piece of cedar shake inside the boot to cover the hole. Most of the men in his company needed replacement clothing and boots, but those items were hard to come by.

It took him a couple of adjustments to get the hat secured on his head, so it didn't hurt the injury to the back of his skull that still pained him. He took a couple of steps away from his dead comrade, and something shiny laying in the grass caught his attention. On the ground a few yards away lay an Arkansas toothpick. He picked up the large knife and lightly ran his thumb along the sharp blade. The pigsticker would come in handy, but he needed a safe way to carry the deadly weapon. He looked around and finally saw a corpse with an empty scabbard attached to a belt around his middle. With his newly acquired knife securely attached around his waist along with two loaded pistols, he began the long walk back to the Rebel camp.

After taking a few steps farther into the woods he reached for his canteen, but it wasn't draped around his neck where he usually carried it. The canteen was one item that a soldier had with him at all times. First he hadn't been able to find his gun or hat, and now his canteen was gone. Maybe he'd been hit on the back of his head at another location, and simply didn't remember crawling to the ditch where he'd woken up. But it didn't matter now where his things were. He needed to turn back and find a couple of canteens to take with him.

He went back where the soldiers lay, leaned over the first one he came to and took the canteen from around his neck. He removed the plug in the top and took long swallows of the lifesaving water. This one was almost empty now, so he went to the next corpse and checked if he had water in his container, but it was empty because of a bullet hole. The third soldier had an almost-full canteen so he took it. As he went down on one knee to check another man, heard a shot to his right. Birds flew out of a tree and headed south.

Sawyer scrambled to the nearest tree and at the same time frantically tried to get one of the guns out. The Army-issued holster had a leather flap covering the gun so it wouldn't fall out, and it seemed to take forever to free the weapon. He hid behind the tree, not knowing where the shot had come from. He stood waiting a few seconds until his breathing calmed. He'd been taught during his early days with Captain Quantrill to play the odds and never confront the enemy when you were outnumbered. Since he didn't know the shooter's location or how many there were, he ran to the next tree and then another.

There were no more shots fired, and he wasn't completely positive it had been intended for him. His instinct told him to retreat and get away as quickly as possible since he was still in the vicinity of the abandoned Union camp. Sooner or later, burial details from both sides would collect their dead and dispose of the corpses. He wanted to be far away when the Bluecoats came after their dead.

Sawyer eased his way through the woods, being careful not to leave any tracks that would be easily followed, until he came to a small branch with running water. He wanted to fill his canteens, but couldn't take the time to do it right then—he needed to keep moving.

When he had walked more than a mile south, he turned west so he could start looking for the rest of his company. He finally stopped beside a creek, filled both of his canteens, and then put his head in the cool water to wash off the back of his skull. The knot was still present, but the pounding pain had subsided a great deal. The cool water felt good on his head. As he was finishing up and getting ready to stand and cross the rocky stream, he heard leaves rustling in the woods. The squirrels that had been playing nearby ran up into trees, warning him of danger. He instantly removed one of his guns and cocked the hammer. Not more than sixty feet away were three Union soldiers coming toward him on foot.

He had to think quickly. His only way out was to draw his second gun and hold his position until he saw what they intended to do. A couple more steps and the men stopped and looked northeast in the direction of the Union camp. All three men started that way, never looking in Sawyer's direction as he squatted beside the creek with a gun in each hand.

That was a close call. But he had been ready to kill the three men and knew that he could have—he had the advantage over them because they hadn't known he was there. They were now walking east so he continued to walk west.

# Chapter Five

Having seen the three Union soldiers on patrol made Sawyer travel slower and keep a watchful eye out for more of the enemy. He stayed in the timber and rocky terrain as much as possible so he wouldn't be seen as easily. By nightfall he still hadn't seen any of his fellow soldiers, and decided to get to higher ground before darkness set in so he could look for their cook fires. Even a small fire would illuminate the darkness and the smoke would trail into the clear sky.

He found a good location close to a grouping of pine trees and sat on the ground to observe the southern and western sky. With no provisions and hunger pangs beginning to take hold in his stomach, he hoped he could find his group soon. Toward the southwest he could see the faint orange glow of a fire, so he started to walk in that direction. The last few months, food and provisions had been hard to come by. The supply wagons that brought the soldiers provisions kept getting attacked by Union fighters and their rations stolen.

There seemed to be a major gap in the supply lines, and there were days that the men had to go without any nourishment.

The terrain became rocky and was covered with so much brush that his clothes kept getting hung up and tearing. He got a whiff of something cooking, which made him want to rush and get to the camp. But he knew better than to hurry. The closer he got, the better he could see the glow of the fire and hear men talking. He waited and listened before moving forward three steps at a time. He was trained to move slowly and stop often to listen, and to stay hidden and blend in with the surroundings. A couple of more steps and he could make out two men sitting on a log with their backs to him.

Sawyer waited and watched, still not knowing if they were his Johnny Rebs or enemy Yankee soldiers. He took a couple more steps forward, like a stalking mountain lion after its prey. Their conversation grew louder the closer he crept, and one of the men got up to check on the two small pots cooking on the fire.

They were Union soldiers, and he had to endure the pain of watching them eat whatever it was they were cooking. He pushed the hunger from his mind like he had so much lately and planned out his attack. He was close enough that he could sneak into their camp when the two men went to sleep and cut their throats. This had been what he was trained to do—spy on his enemy and neutralize any and all threats.

He continued to watch the men finish their supper. One of the men poured the contents of one pot into the other one and placed a rag over it so bugs would stay out. The other soldier took the empty pot into the woods south of their fire, and came back in a few minutes, appearing to have cleaned it. Sawyer figured there was a spring or creek close by. Both men put their meager bedding on the ground where they were going to sleep and got ready for bed.

Sawyer waited patiently, giving the men time to drift off into a deep sleep before he tried anything. He contemplated what he was going to do with them. His first thought was to sneak in and cut their throats and let them bleed to death. But then again, this wasn't really the heat of battle. Maybe he should go in and hold them at gunpoint as he took what he wanted.

Their snoring grew steady—it was time to make his move. He carefully placed each step so his sounds wouldn't wake up his prey. With a pistol in each hand so he could cover both men at the same time, he pulled back the hammers in unison. The metal clashing of the hammers brought one of the men awake, but before he could do anything, Sawyer spoke.

"I've got you covered, so lay still and don't move." The Union soldier, who was no more than a boy, looked up at the barrel of the Colt aimed at him.

"Yes sir, I ain't moving one bit."

The other man lifted his head. "What in tarnation is going on?"

"Shut up and do what you're told," said the first man.

"I'm tired and hungry. If you cooperate and don't give me any lip, then I'll let you live," said Sawyer.

"Mister, we're just trying to get back to our camp northeast of here. We were attacked early this morning and have been chasing Rebels all day," said one of the men. "But no offense to you, since you fight for the South."

"None taken. Now I want you to get up one at a time and strip, and then lie on your stomach."

"I ain't taking off my clothes," said the younger of the two.

"Fine," said Sawyer. "I'll just cut your throat and then I won't have to worry about you coming looking for me."

"Since you explained it that way, I think I'll do what you said." The young soldier removed all his clothes down to his long john underwear.

"That's enough. Now lie down and put your hands behind your back. Do either of you have any rope in your supplies?" asked Sawyer.

"Yeah, we have some short pieces of rope we use to secure our tents," said the man still clothed.

"Where is it?"

"Right here in my pouch," said the man, and he reached for a bag that lay on the ground next to him.

Sawyer moved closer to the soldier and touched the gun to the side of his head. "You pull out that rope and nothing else, and I suggest that you move slow as molasses in the winter."

The soldier eased his hand to the bag, pulled the flap open, and stuck his hand inside. Sawyer could see him moving his hand around, searching for the rope.

"Don't shoot, I'm goin' to bring my hand out now."

"You better not have anything in it except the cord," said Sawyer.

The soldier showed him the rope.

"I want you to tie your partner's hands behind his back, good and tight. I'll be watching, so no fast moves."

The man nodded his head, leaned over, and began to tie up his fellow soldier. When he finished, Sawyer said, "It's your turn now, so get undressed and lie down."

"Mister, I ain't got no drawers on."

"That's too bad. I guess you better do as I say and hope that I get finished here quick before the bugs and worms begin to feed on you."

The man did as instructed and lay on his stomach, naked. Sawyer put a knee against his backside and tied the man's hands behind his back. When he finished, he sat down and ate from the pot full of food. It contained stewed rabbit, wild onions, and turnips, cooked in water. Sawyer hated the taste of turnips, but he ate them anyway since he had gone two days without a meal. When he finished eating, he gathered up his things and searched through the two soldiers' pockets and gear. Both men lay on the ground not four feet away and watched as he looked over their things. He finished his search and went where the two captives lay.

"I'm leaving now to go find the rest of my group. I don't reckon you fellers know where they might be, do you?"

One of the men rolled over on his side. "The last we heard, them Johnny Rebs were hightailing it due west toward the Current River with their tails between their legs."

"Is that a fact?" asked Sawyer. "You don't see me running, do you?"

"Don't take what he said personal," said the other man as he squirmed on the ground where he could see Sawyer's face. "He didn't mean you at all, did you, Homer?"

"No, I didn't mean that toward you. You've treated us admirably and we appreciate you not killing us."

"Well, now that I have your attention again, don't try to follow me. I won't be so nice next time we meet." Sawyer began to walk west and never looked back at the two men.

# Chapter Six

Darkness set in for the evening and he had no idea where he would bed down that night. This was unfamiliar territory to him, and all he could hope for now was to find a farm and try to use their barn, since he had no sleeping gear.

Something one of the Union soldiers had said bothered him, and he wished that he had questioned the man and gotten details. They'd said that the last they'd heard, the Johnny Rebs were heading west toward the Current River with their tails tucked between their legs. Did that mean that a larger Union force was out here, engaging his company of soldiers and picking them off? If that's what had happened, he hoped they had given up the hunt and returned to their camp by now. He didn't want a confrontation with a large number of soldiers; he'd have no chance of survival. It would be his death warrant. The one thing in his favor was that he would be able to see them before they saw him. Wherever they were bedded down for the night, they'd have campfires scattered around for cooking.

By the location of the moon, he surmised that it was after midnight. He was dead tired and needed sleep. It had gotten difficult to find his way through the rocks, cliffs, and mountainous terrain of North Central Arkansas. At least he wouldn't have to worry about that when he returned to Kansas after the war ended. The flat farmland of his home state seemed like a lifetime away to the young man.

He pushed himself to continue, negotiating his way up a small mountain. The footing happened to be good, and he had trees to hold on to for support. When he reached the crest, he sat on the ground with his back to a tree, catching his breath and letting his tired legs rest. Through the trees he thought he could see a clearing, and it appeared from the faint light of the moon that some animals were grazing there. He wanted to sit where he was and sleep, but he needed to check out what was in that opening. It could be Union cavalry horses chomping on grass, and if that was the case then their camp was here.

He pulled his tired body up and eased through the trees so he had a better view of the clearing. Cows lay on the ground chewing their cud, while others were eating grass. Four hundred yards farther west was what looked like a house and barn.

Sawyer made his way to the barn without incident and went inside to find the ladder leading to the hayloft. He climbed up the ladder and ruffled up a good bed of the straw, and that was as far as he got. He lay on the hay and went to sleep.

Sun rays shining through the gaps in the boards on the east side of the barn warmed the young soldier's face, forcing him to open his eyes. Sawyer yawned and stretched, not wanting to get up yet as he put a hand over his eyes to block the bright sunlight.

"I've got a double-barrel shotgun. Who's up there?" shouted someone below in the barn.

He felt stupid for not being more careful. All his training and he had let some farmer sneak up on him in the barn. He reached to his holster and removed one of his pistols. "Don't shoot! I'm Sawyer McCade and I'm a soldier getting some sleep in your hayloft."

"You a Yank or Reb?"

"I'm a Confederate soldier passing through, trying to find my detachment somewhere west of here."

"Come on down and make yourself at home in the barn while I go to the house and get you some food. I'm Daniel Westbrook, and this is my farm. You can't be seen here since we've seeing patrols of Yankee soldiers for the past three days."

Sawyer made his way to the ladder and cautiously looked over the edge of the loft to see a man in his sixties standing looking up at him. The shotgun was leaned against the wall, so Sawyer climbed down to the ground.

"Thanks for the benefit of your barn and offer of food, Mr. Westbrook. I got hit on the back of my head night before last and became separated from my unit. I'm wondering if you've seen them pass by or heard any news of them in these parts?"

"No, I ain't seen hide nor hair of any Confederate soldiers around here, but I haven't been off the farm in a month. You stay out of sight, and I'll go to the house and get you the ham and biscuits that's left over from breakfast."

"Yes sir, I'll find me a seat and stay right here. I never turn down food, especially biscuits."

Daniel smiled at Sawyer's remark and took hold of the barrel of his shotgun. "I'll take this with me in case some Bluecoats happen to ride through without warning. They do that some, you know."

"You don't say," replied Sawyer, getting suspicious of the man now. "How often do you see the soldiers?"

"It's not uncommon to see some every few days, I reckon," said Daniel.

"Do they stop and talk to you when they come through?"

The man looked a little nervous and he began to get fidgety. Sawyer could tell he was wanting to go to the house and end the conversation.

"They've stopped in the past, but not lately. They think that I support the North, but I have them fooled. I go around the farm singing 'I Wish I Was in the Land of Dixie' all the time. I best be going to get that food so you can eat and then rest some more until dark."

"Yeah, you probably should. I'm really hungry and the rest will do me good. You go on ahead and I'll stay hidden," said Sawyer.

Daniel took his shotgun with him and left the barn. Sawyer went to the wall and watched through a crack in the boards as the man walked to the house. He saw Daniel turn and look back at the barn before entering his house.

Five minutes later, the man started toward the barn with a bucket in his hand. About the time that Daniel was at the barn door, a woman came out the front door of the house and lay a red blanket over a section of fence that surrounded the small front yard. She then stood looking to the north for a few seconds before going back into the house.

The woman's actions warned Sawyer that something wasn't right. The situation wasn't what the man wanted him to believe. Maybe she had signaled someone that they had company. Most likely she put the red blanket on the fence so Union soldiers could see her warning. He'd play dumb, eat their food, and make them think he would stay hidden until dark. Instead, he would eat and sneak out before they knew he was gone.

"Boy, where are you? I've got you the rest of our breakfast."

"I'm right here behind you," said Sawyer as he stepped out from the side of the door frame. "I sure appreciate the food, hospitality, and place to hide out until dark. If it's okay with you, I'll take that bucket you're holding and go over there." Sawyer pointed to a log bench where he could sit to eat and rest.

"Here's your food. I'll get you more later when the wife cooks dinner. You go ahead and fill up that stomach. I'll be back later."

Sawyer sat down and began to eat the biscuits with ham and drink from his canteen. As soon as Daniel closed the barn door, Sawyer went back to the barn wall and watched the man hurry to the house. Daniel kept looking back at the barn and then to the north.

It was time to run. Those troops that the Westbrooks had alerted would be here soon. He gathered up his things and tried to open the door, but it wouldn't budge. He shook his head. That old coot thought a lock on the door could keep him from running.

With his canteens around his neck and shoulders, he walked along the walls of the barn until he came

# Life After War

upon a grouping of loose boards. He didn't want to kick them off or break them, so he searched the man's tool chest and found a crowbar that he could use to remove the boards. The old boards were easy to pry open enough for him to pass through. At six-foot-two and weighing 165 pounds, he managed to get enough of an opening that he could escape the barn. It was risky to put the boards back in place the best he could so that it wasn't obvious where he exited the barn. He started off in a southeast direction so the people in the house wouldn't see him because the barn had him hidden from their sight. When he arrived at the woods, he changed his direction and walked west.

He stayed close enough to the open field so he could watch the house. Hopefully he'd be far away before the soldiers arrived. He smiled to himself; they would spend valuable time inside the barn looking for him. He'd have no remorse if the soldiers decided to punish the Westbrooks for his escape. That would be on the Westbrooks, as they most likely played both sides of the conflict, depending on which side paid them the most.

25

# Chapter Seven

Sawyer hurried through the woods as fast as he could, trying not to make too much noise or draw attention to his location. He kept a watchful eye out for additional Union soldiers who could be in the vicinity of the Westbrooks' farm. He expected to at least hear soldiers scurrying around the countryside searching for his trail, but he knew how to operate so that any sign he left would blend in with the environment.

Confederate scouts were trained to be as invisible as possible and take their enemy by surprise. If soldiers were sent after him, it would be a group of no more than five men and most likely only three, since he was alone and not an officer who might know important information. He could probably take three men with his knife and not have to fire a shot.

The fast pace he kept through the rough terrain tired him out in less than an hour. He estimated that he had most likely traveled three miles since leaving the farm and it was time for a break. It appeared that he was on high ground, and he had a good view of the surrounding area. Still, he didn't want to take any chances, so he lay one of his guns in his lap as he sat on the ground and leaned against a tree. He took long sips of water from one of his canteens until it was almost empty, and his thirst subsided. One of the biscuits that Daniel had brought him was in his powder bag, and he ate the cold bread and washed it down with a little more water. Now one canteen empty and he needed to watch for a water source to replenish his supply.

His body ached, and he needed to cool off and rest. He fell asleep leaning against the tree trunk, only to be awakened by the sound of metal striking a rock. He peeked around the tree trunk to see two soldiers on horses coming his way. They rode in single file with rifles resting across their saddles, the barrel in the crook of their arm. It so happened that his back was to the riders, and they didn't see the young soldier as he peered at them from the tree.

A horse's hoof struck another rock with its metal shoe, but Sawyer stayed still. He moved his hand to the gun in his lap and unwearyingly waited in case he had to kill. Since they hadn't seen him yet, it was a good possibility that they would keep riding. His head still hurt from his injury, and he wanted nothing more than to move his head from resting against the tree. But patience was a key skill in battle, and even though his head hurt, he had to stay still until the soldiers were farther away.

The Union soldiers kept riding north, the opposite of the direction he needed to go. When he thought it was safe, he stood up. They were out of sight and he couldn't hear them anymore, but in case there were more of them he kept the Colt out and carried it in his hand, ready to fire.

Sawyer walked south through the forest, rocks, and brush so he could put some distance between him and the two soldiers. An hour later he turned west, hoping that the soldiers hadn't changed their directions but kept riding north.

Later that afternoon, he squeezed his way between two large boulders that partially blocked his trail and walked into a camp. Two Union soldiers sat on the ground eating jerky, but jumped up when they saw him. They started to raise their rifles to shoot, but Sawyer drew his gun and fired. The first man took lead in the chest and fell backward. The second man cocked his rifle and fired, but the shot went wide to the right of Sawyer. The second Union soldier never had a chance after that—the ball from the pistol hit him in the forehead. Gunpowder smoke filled the air and trailed from the barrel of both guns. The two horses tied up nearby in some trees nickered and pulled against the bridle reins but settled down once the shooting stopped. Sawyer saw them out of the corner of his eyes but left them be until he was certain he'd dealt with the soldiers.

Both Union soldiers were dead when Sawyer went to them and checked for a heartbeat. The only thing of use he found when he rummaged through their pockets were three dollars in Union Greenbacks and what jerky they had left. He took his time and reloaded the two spent bullets from his gun before he pulled the men close together and piled up rocks and tree limbs to cover the corpses. This was something he usually didn't do in battle; in most instances he didn't care what happened to the corpses. For some unknown reason, today was different.

It was hard work covering up the dead men and he needed a break, so he sat down on a rock, drank some water, then ate jerky. It was a good day. He now had horses to ride and could get back with his unit faster and easier. After resting and eating, he untied both horses and headed out. Riding a horse was so much better than walking, especially when he had worn-out boots and the rough terrain. He could cover a lot more ground and wouldn't be so tired at the end of the day.

By the time the sun began to set in the west, Sawyer found a large rock overhang that would give him shelter during the night. He removed the Ranger saddles off both horses and used one of them along with the two saddle blankets to sleep on. Tied to the saddle on the extra horse had been a bag, and inside it were two potatoes, an onion, and a small frying pan.

The horses were hobbled and couldn't leave his camp. He gathered firewood to cook his meal. Thunder rumbled far away to the southwest, and it would probably rain before the night was over. But the overhang would provide him ample cover. With no rain slicker to protect him from the cold downpour, he would have to stay hunkered down under his shelter.

He made his campfire as far back under the rock ledge as possible so the rain wouldn't get to it and put it out. With his fire close to the rock wall, it would also give him radiant heat as the flames ricocheted off the rock. He hoped the storm would pass quickly and only last a few hours, as opposed to raining for days.

Sometime after midnight the rain started, and occasionally lightning struck in the vicinity. He woke up a little cold and added more sticks to the few coals that were still smoldering. Blowing on the red coals got them flaming again, and he felt warmer as the flames grew bigger. He wasn't worried about anyone seeing his fire in the storm and moved his bed closer to the warm rock wall.

Sawyer lay on his bed of two saddle blankets and thought about the day he joined the Confederate army along with his friends and the glory they would share together when the war would be over. They never discussed getting shot or dying on the battlefield. Now here he was hiding out, trying to find his unit and stay clear of Union soldiers. Both of his friends were dead, and he had killed countless men over the past two years. His life as a soldier was not glamorous or remarkable by any stretch of the imagination. Yes, he was a fighter and sometimes a cold-blooded killer, but in war those weren't considered bad things. In fact, most fellow soldiers and officers commended him on his abilities. The glory he had thought about when he joined up was nothing more than the memory of a kid. There was no glory in killing.

Based on the reports from the field and the lack of supplies and reinforcements most units experienced, it was a consensus belief among his fellow soldiers that the Confederate States were losing the war. It seemed that they were on the run, retreating with every battle, and that was a bad omen.

Daylight brought with it drizzle left over from the early morning storm. Both horses were still in the general area of the camp, grazing on the green but sparse grass. Sawyer had removed the gun holsters from around his waist before he'd gone to sleep and covered

the guns with part of the saddle blanket to keep moisture out of the powder. Now he examined the holsters
and wanted to cut the flap off them, so he could get the
guns out faster. The knife he'd taken off the dead
soldier came in handy as he sliced through the leather
with ease.

When he finally finished modifying one holster, he
stood up and put it on. He practiced drawing the
weapon. It was a much faster and smoother process
than before. He sat back down and did the same to the
other holster. Then he cut two latigos off the spare
saddle to make safety straps so the guns wouldn't fall
out unexpectedly. By the time he finished working on
the holsters, the drizzle had stopped, although it was
still cloudy. He saddled his horses and broke camp,
heading on west.

# Chapter Eight

That day he rode approximately ten miles over rough terrain, stopping at a stream to water his horses and rest. Hunger pangs were setting in since he hadn't eaten anything since the day before. As he rested, he gazed at the clear stream he sat next to while his horses drank the cool water and grazed. Numerous trout swam in the shallow water, and it seemed like they kept going back and forth in one spot. He removed his boots and britches before stepping into the cool water. He watched the fish, trying to see if they swam in a particular area of the creek.

Moving slowly so he wouldn't scare the fish away, he made it to the far bank. There he saw a big group of trout whirl by, so he stood with his legs slightly apart, bent over with his hands in the water. He watched and waited for a few minutes, until finally a trout rushed up to his hands. As it started through the opening, he closed his hands around the fish and caught it. The trout was about fourteen inches long and would make a fine meal.

As he ate, Sawyer reflected on his life before he had joined the army. Life had been hard growing up on a large farm where it was just his parents, sister and himself to do all the work. They had to get up at four each morning and milk five cows. After breakfast it was the same every day. Go to the fields and either plow, plant, or harvest. He hated farming and wanted to get away so badly that he and his friends had joined the army. What a mistake that had been.

Farm life didn't look so bad now that he never knew when he might be shot at or have to kill someone. There were days that he didn't eat or have a bed to sleep in. The good things he remembered about living on the farm were sleeping in a soft bed, three delicious meals every day, and he never had to wear clothes that were ragged and torn. His ma worked hard every day as the house cook, cleaning and washing clothes. His sister was a little older than him and she helped his ma with the cooking, but she also had to work in the fields at times. He missed his sister and loved her very much. No, farming wasn't so bad after all, and he was ready for this war to be over so he could get back to his family.

He needed to move on and put more miles behind him. If all went as he hoped, he would start seeing signs of his detachment soon. He couldn't be more than fifty miles from the Current River the Union soldiers said his detachment was heading for, although he might have to ride up or downstream to find them.

A few more miles of riding and he came to a road that ran in a westward direction. There were many horse tracks and wagon ruts in the dirt. The road had to be used as a military route to the river. Hopefully he wouldn't encounter any Union soldiers as he urged his horses into a lope and hurried down the path.

He made remarkable time and distance on the road; it was so much easier than having to fight through the rocks and trees in the forest. He passed by a few travelers and was feeling good about the progress until he rounded a curve that skirted a large outcropping of boulders. His previous battlefield training kicked in and he dropped the reins of his spare horse to draw his right-handed gun. A small tree with its branches cut off about a foot from the main part of the tree lay across the road that was used to stop travelers so the soldiers could stop and inspect the voyagers before letting them proceed down the road.

Five soldiers stood guard with their rifles in their hands when the rider with two horses came upon them. Sawyer fired at the men as he came charging up to their location, not giving them time to draw a good bead on him. The surprised soldiers fired in his direction but were shooting wild. Three of them went down as he fired shot after shot. His horse leaped over the tree, and he passed by their checkpoint. The gun hammer clicked on an empty chamber, so he put it back into its holster and pulled out the other one, jerking the reins to the left. His horse turned around and Sawyer started back toward the remaining soldiers, who were shooting at him now. He leaned as far as he could over the horse's neck and fired at the men as he rode past them, then turned the horse once more and fired until all five men were on the ground.

Sawyer dismounted and saw his spare horse dead on the side of the road. He decided to reload each of his guns before he approached the dead men to search their pockets and see if they had anything he could use. Reloading his guns still took more time than he wanted, but he had to be ready to shoot again if more soldiers were close by. It took him a couple of minutes before he had them fully loaded and back into their holsters. He drew the Arkansas toothpick knife and searched the first man and then the next. When he came to the fourth man, the soldier moaned and tried to open his eyes. Sawyer sliced through the jugular vein on the man's neck and finished him off. This was war, and he wasn't taking any chances of one of them shooting him in the back or taking him as a prisoner.

In all, he removed nine dollars off the men and more gunpowder. There was food in the way of jerky, hardtack and two cans of beans. He transferred what food he found to one sack and took off on his horse. The checkpoint meant there were a lot more soldiers close by, and he had to get off the road quickly until he could figure out their location.

After a short distance of a fourth of a mile, he left the road and rode west through sparse timber and found a lush, green valley close to a half mile wide and a mile long. On both sides of the basin were steep-sided mountains that would be hard for a horse to climb. A quarter of a mile into the valley, he saw to his right a wild animal trail zigzagging up the side of one of the mountains, so he followed, hoping it would take him high enough to be able to see what lay ahead of him. He had to stop twice and let his horse rest before they made it to the peak.

As he neared the crest of the mountain, he heard gunfire farther west. The firing seemed to be sporadic—perhaps there was a skirmish taking place. The ridge of the mountain was running in an east–west direction toward the Current River. As he looked toward the west, he couldn't see an encampment or anything that resembled a camp because of the trees and other foliage.

It was impossible to tell what lay ahead or what danger posed a threat for him. He nudged his horse forward and stayed on top of the ridge until it started to slope back into the valley up ahead. The sound of gunfire was getting closer, but he couldn't pinpoint where it was coming from. He found a clear path down off the mountain and continued west on better terrain where the land was now grass running up and down gentle, rolling hills.

A creek flowed clear water through the west edge of the valley, so Sawyer followed it, knowing that it would most likely take him to the Current River or to another creek that ran into the river. He rode on with a gun in his right hand, expecting trouble at any moment. But it never came, and he reached the banks of the swift-running Current River without incident. The rain from the night before had caused the water to rise until it was bank full.

The sporadic shooting could be heard, but now it was south of his location and seemed to be along the waterway. He urged his horse toward the sounds, but rode carefully with the reins in his left hand and his gun in the right in case he ran into soldiers on the way. The terrain along the river was so poor that it took him two hours to travel two miles downstream. He had to worm his way around boulders, through deep ravines, and find clear paths through the pine and hardwood trees.

Stopping his horse at the edge of a tree-covered hill,

he could finally see the holler where the fighting was taking place. It was in a small valley between two hills that ran toward the river. It looked like there were at most twenty to thirty Confederate troops dug in behind trees and rocks, fighting off a smaller Union patrol of a dozen well-placed men who had the Rebs surrounded.

Dead ahead were six Union soldiers, crouched behind a grouping of rocks. He turned around and went back into the trees, riding east about a hundred yards before turning back to observe the fighting once more. He was now behind the six Yankee soldiers, and if he came out of the trees riding hard, he could overtake them and hopefully shoot most of them before he'd have to retreat to reload his guns.

With a gun in each hand, Sawyer lined his horse up and wrapped the bridle reins around the saddle horn. He kicked the horse hard and let it run toward the men, while he used his legs and knees against the horse's side to guide the animal toward the Union soldiers.

This was the kind of guerrilla fighting Sawyer had been trained for, and his unexpected advancement took the Union soldiers by surprise. He was upon them before they knew he was coming, and as they turned toward him, he was already firing his guns. Three men died as he rode through their guard. He turned his horse around and came back through their defense, shooting two more men before riding back into trees to take cover and reload his pistols.

With two fully loaded guns, he rode farther east and then turned south to come in behind another group of Yankee fighters. This time he had to wait until there were gunshots coming from inside the trees because he couldn't see the exact location of the soldiers. As the shooting started back up, he couldn't see the soldiers, but he could see the plumes of smoke from the barrels of their guns when they fired.

Once he'd located the three men, he dismounted and tied his horse to a tree limb and proceeded on foot to their location. He was able to sneak in so close that he removed his knife and used it on the first soldier while the other two fired at the Confederate troops. They were unaware of his presence and were reloading their muzzle loaders when he shot both of the remaining two men. He searched their pockets to find only two dollars between the three soldiers. It was time to go back for his horse and make sure no more Union troops were hiding out waiting to shoot him. He rode where he could get a good view of the surrounding area.

Someone or something made a lot of noise as they crashed through the leaves off to his left. He kept his position until he spotted a soldier hunched over, trying to sneak out of the battle. Sawyer drew his knife and stood still behind the tree he'd been using for conceal-ment. He heard the man pass by him and, with one lunge, wheeled around the tree and stuck the knife through the man's left side, hitting his heart. The man gave out a grunt as he went to the ground, dead. Sawyer bent down, removed the knife, and wiped the blade clean on the man's shirt. He went through his pockets and found two silver dollars.

The shooting had all but stopped, with nine of the Union soldiers dead. Sawyer went to his horse and rode north, circling back to where he had killed the first five men. Hopeful of finding food, he turned the first man over...but then heard a faint sound behind him. With the Colt in his hand, he turned to see a soldier coming up behind him. One shot from his gun and the man went down. The wounded man tried to get back up, but Sawyer was already on him and sliced through his neck with the knife.

He searched through the pockets of the now six soldiers and found a small amount of money on each one. He mounted up and went back into the woods to observe the defensive position of the Union patrol for more movement. After thirty minutes, there had been no more gunfire. Either the remaining soldiers had decided to leave, or they were lying in wait for him to ride by.

He decided to ride back east a little way and look for the remaining retreating soldiers. Sure enough, when he had covered a half mile, he got a glimpse of them as they retreated to the east away from his location.

Sawyer turned and rode back where his own men were hunkered down in the valley, wounded and hungry.

# Chapter Nine

"Hello! It's Sergeant Sawyer McCade. I'm riding in, so hold your fire." A ragtag group of fifteen or so soldiers emerged from behind cover. The first thing he noticed was some of the men didn't have any type of weapon. They looked like they had been ridden hard and put up wet, judging by the shape they were in. Some had makeshift bandages on different parts of their bodies and most of the men looked like they were so tired they could hardly stand.

"Come on in, Sergeant, we ain't got enough ammunition to shoot you anyway," said one of the soldiers. "Those Yanks were about to end the fight for us. We've been pinned down here for two days without any food, and almost all our gunpowder and lead are gone."

"Who are you, and where is the rest of the Third Army?" asked Sawyer.

The soldier came out from behind a tree. "I'm Corporal William Boatwright. We got cut off from the main regiment. The infantry and light artillery units are farther down the river toward Ivey's Ford heading to

Clarksville. They're supposed to join up with the cavalry units there for a big battle."

"I killed nine Union soldiers by those trees." Sawyer pointed in the direction he came in from. "I suggest some of your able-bodied men go over there and get their guns and what gunpowder and lead shot they have on them. We may need it before we get connected back up with the main unit."

"We need food and rest," said Boatwright. "We've been hunkered down without any nourishment and little water. The Yankees hit us hard and this unit got separated from the main command when the fighting started. We lost close to a hundred men in these hills the past few days."

"For now, send some men to get those rifles and what ammunition they have. Those soldiers may have some food on them also, so have them bring back anything they can use. In the meantime, I'll scout around the area and make sure the enemy have left. Hopefully I'll see a deer or two. I left a dead horse back about two miles north on the road, where the soldiers had a checkpoint. You may want to send some of your men to butcher the horse and cook him tonight. Even though I'm not fond of horsemeat, it'll do when there's nothing else available," said Sawyer.

"That may be our best option for today. With the shooting here over the last two days, I'd be surprised if there's a deer within five miles of this location. I'll assign a few men to find the horse and have some others search the soldiers. I assume the soldiers at the checkpoint are also dead and have rifles and ammo."

"Yes, they do. I'll go ahead and scout the area and

meet up with your men at the dead animal. We can carry the meat back on my horse," said Sawyer.

"Thanks, Sergeant. I'll get the men started that way. You look toward the east for more Bluecoats. They may be sending reinforcements to finish us off. That's the direction they been coming from."

Sawyer mounted up and rode west until he came to the river. It was only another five hundred yards from where he'd found the troops. He then turned southeast to skirt around the hills and mountains that he had crossed earlier. Off to the east he thought he saw smoke, but couldn't be sure. In any case, it was so far away that it probably wasn't a concern.

By the time he rode up to the Union checkpoint, the men that Corporal Boatright had sent to find the dead horse had already started cutting off large chunks of meat from the animal. Sawyer found a couple of small tents in the woods nearby, and they used the canvas to wrap the meat so it could be hung off both sides of his saddle. He walked on foot with the under-nourished men until they got back to the makeshift camp close to the river.

The men who were injured had stayed in camp and built three fires to cook the meat on when the rest of the unit returned. The coals were spread out, and a few soldiers cut slices of meat and cooked it in a frying pan on the hot coals. The hungry soldiers went after the meat like wild animals until they had their bellies full.

When everyone had finally stopped eating, Sawyer asked for their attention. "Men, we have rifles and ammo, so I want you to get some rest tonight because tomorrow we head south downstream to find the rest of our detachment. I think it's best we stay close to the river, even though we'll be plodding through some rough terrain. I'll go out in front and try to find us a good path through here and be on the lookout for wildlife that we can eat. I'll need one of the rifles to take with me. If I shoot something, I'll leave it on the trail where you can find it."

"I'm familiar with this area, and I do believe that there's a road we can take that's four miles or so east of the river," said Corporal Boatwright. "If we stay on that road and keep in a southward direction, we'll have a lot better footing. It's mostly farmland and the road will lead all the way to Little Rock. There we can turn due west and ride to Clarksville."

"That's fine with me. I'm from the flat plains of Kansas, and don't like rocks and mountains anyway. I'll ride that way and see if I can find the road. We may get lucky and get food on the way to Little Rock from some sympathetic supporters," said Sawyer.

With the rest of the horsemeat cooked for breakfast that next morning, the ragged troops headed southeast toward the road that Corporal Boatwright thought he remembered. Sawyer went ahead on his horse and found the path about four miles in front of the men. He kept riding south on the road until he saw fields filled with Black workers tending to the crops. He didn't think anyone should be a slave, even though he fought for the South. In Kansas, his folks didn't use slave labor and they were sympathetic to the Union. He only joined the Confederate army because his friends did. He now wished he had stayed on the farm and kept working.

It had been a long three years, and he was tired of all the killing and not having proper sleeping conditions

43

or decent food to eat. It seemed like the longer the war carried on, the worse the conditions became. He didn't know how the fighting in other parts of the country was going, but it seemed like here, they were getting overcome and having to retreat more often.

The first day on the road, one of the wounded soldiers died. They stopped long enough to find a place to lay his body and cover it with rocks so the wild animals and buzzards wouldn't get to it. One of the soldiers made a crude wooden cross out of two sticks lashed together with string.

Even though they were on a smooth road, it was still rough going while traveling with wounded men. They had to stop often for rest. Sawyer stayed with the group and finally dismounted and had the men cut two long poles so they could make a drag sled. That way, the most injured soldiers could take turns getting some rest.

"I think a couple of you should walk beside the sled and make sure no one falls off. I'm going on ahead to find us food and a place to hold up for the night. If you hear gunfire, take cover and wait on me," said Sawyer.

"Sergeant, I'm Ronnie Bristow from down Texas way. I was wondering if I could take point with you in case you run into trouble," said the young soldier as he walked up to Sawyer.

"Sure, come on, Ronnie. I'm hoping we can find a farm where we're welcome and can get provisions and rest. Most of these men are in bad shape and need nourishment and rest so they can make the long trip to find the rest of our company. I don't know how far it is to Clarksville, but I suspect it's more than a couple hundred miles. You take the right side of the road and I'll take the left."

The two soldiers walked along each side of the road and could see fields with people working in them. They weren't sure where they were, but they had gotten away from the mountainous area and were in farm and pastureland somewhere northeast of the capital, Little Rock.

As they continued south, they came to a field planted in crops with numerous weeds throughout the rows. Ronnie spoke. "Sawyer, something don't seem quite up to par here."

"What do you mean? I don't see anything wrong," replied Sawyer, a little bewildered.

"The other fields we passed by have people working in them," said Ronnie, pointing back behind him. "But this particular field"—he pointed to his right— "ain't got no one in it, and it don't look like it's seen any workers in a long while. I think we should find the farmhouse and have us a look-see. Maybe it's abandoned and could be a good place to hold up for a while."

"I hadn't noticed that, but you might be right. I'm thinking we keep walking, but keep your weapon ready to fire, and see if we can spot some buildings. It sure would be nice if there was someplace we could use for shelter and get food along here somewhere," said Sawyer.

A quarter of a mile farther south, Ronnie pointed east. "Look over there by the trees. There's a house and barn. We should go check it out."

"Yeah, but you be ready to use that rifle if we have trouble. I'll swing around to the south and come in from behind the house," said Sawyer as he pulled one of his pistols. "Give me a few minutes to get into position before you come in from the front."

Sawyer walked in a semicircle until he came to the back of the house. He heard Ronnie call out to whoever was inside. Sawyer ran to the back door and kicked it in, only to be hit in the face with the smell of rotten human remains. He stumbled back outside and threw up. The smell of decayed flesh was one thing that made Sawyer sick to his stomach every time he got a good whiff of it.

"Holy crap!" called out Ronnie from inside the house. He came out the back door with his hand over his mouth and nose. "I guess we know why the fields look unkept. These folks have been dead a month or so."

Sawyer stood up and wiped off his mouth. "I reckon so. It's a mess in there. What do you suppose we do about it?"

"I don't rightly know at this point. I'm afraid the bodies will pull apart if we try to move them. Maybe I can find a rag to go over my nose and see if they have any canned food inside. We can always set up camp behind the house if need be," said Ronnie as he looked out over the backyard.

"I tell you what," said Sawyer. "You look for a root cellar and I'll look in the barn. If we don't have to go back into the house, I would say we leave it closed up and use the barn if we can. The best thing for the house is to burn it down when we leave."

"That's a good idea, but don't be surprised if there are more dead bodies in the barn," said Ronnie.

Sawyer was apprehensive when he opened the barn door. He expected to find more decayed bodies but there weren't any. He looked in each stall and in the tack room, only to find everything in order, like whoever had used it had taken care of their things.

He opened the barn's back doors onto a corral, and next to it was a fenced lot with five cows and four horses. The livestock looked to be in solid shape. He stood nodding his head at their good fortune—they now had beef and more horses to use. This was really a blessing, and if he guessed correctly, there would be a wagon around somewhere.

He was correct. Sitting under the lean-to on the side of the barn was a wagon, and it looked to be in good condition. Now if Ronnie had any luck and found canned food in the root cellar or somewhere else, the men would be able to rest up here for a few days, regain some of their strength and be in much better health to travel.

# Chapter Ten

"Ronnie, where're you at?" asked Sawyer as he left the barn.

"I'm over here behind this old smokehouse," hollered Ronnie. He went to the corner and waved his arms in the air so Sawyer could see him.

Sawyer walked over to a small building and found the young soldier coming back out of a cellar with two half-gallon jars of green beans and potatoes. He had already placed a dozen jars full of canned vegetables on the ground.

"The cellar is full of canned goods," said Ronnie.

"Good. We're in luck, there're five cows out behind the barn in a small field. I also saw four horses and a wagon that the weak and injured can ride in when we leave," said Sawyer. "I saw a stack of tarpaulins in the barn. Do you think we can put enough covers on the corpses to cut down on the smell long enough to get the cookware out of the house?"

Ronnie thought for a few moments, then said, "We should be able to cover them up and open some windows to let the house air out enough that it's tolerable inside."

"Okay, I'll go back to the barn and collect whatever I can find to cover them with."

Sawyer came out of the barn with his arms full of canvases and took them to the back porch. Ronnie had the front and back doors open and the putrid smell was everywhere.

Ronnie handed Sawyer a large piece of wet cloth. "Tie this around your face. It'll help with the smell. We'll go in and layer the canvases over the bodies until we run out of material."

Sawyer took the wet cloth and tied it around his face. He was not looking forward to going back into that house. "Let's unfold the canvas out here. That way when we go in, we can just lay it over the bodies."

"Good idea. Here, grab ahold and let's see how big they are. We'll use the smallest first," said Ronnie.

They spread out the tarps, stacked three on top of each other, and then picked them up by the ends and proceeded into the house. When the tarps were on top of the decomposed corpses, they went back outside and took in deep breaths of fresh air. Sawyer stood bent over, spitting on the ground, and almost puked for the second time. He moved farther away from the back door where he could breathe without the smell of dead people.

"To heck with raising the windows. Grab something sturdy and go around that side of the house to break out the glass, and I'll do the same on the other side," said Sawyer.

The sound of glass shattering filled the house. "One of us should go back to the road," said Ronnie. "The men will be coming along soon, and we need to head them this way. That will give the house time to air out some also."

"You go on ahead. I'm going to get one of those cows in closer to the barn so we can butcher it. By that time, I should be able to go back into the house without it smelling too bad."

"Okay, I'll be back directly."

# Chapter Eleven

Sawyer went to the pasture and drove one of the cows toward the barn. Since she wasn't used to him, she kept trying to turn back and regroup with the other cows. Getting frustrated, he decided to check for a rope in the barn. He didn't see any hanging by the stalls, so he went into the tack room next. There were ropes and he also noticed a nice-looking saddle and bridle. Why chase after the cow on foot when he could use a horse?

The horses were gentler than the cows and he was able to walk up to a nice-looking pony. Sawyer rubbed behind the animal's ears and talked to him for a few seconds before he slipped the bridle onto its head. He led the pony to the barn, saddled him up, and mounted. Then he took off after the cows. They were much easier to get back to the barn with the horse. Sawyer liked the pony; he could tell by the way it handled that it had been trained to herd cattle.

By the time he had the cow penned by itself, Ronnie was coming back with the rest of the troops. Sawyer sat on the horse, watching the men hobble toward the barn. These men needed rest and food before they would be able to defend themselves.

"Ronnie, I think you should have four of the strongest men go into the kitchen and haul that cook stove out here into the backyard. It'll be much easier to dry meat for jerky and cook on than an open fire."

"I agree. Have you been inside since we busted out the windows and opened the doors?"

"No, but I'm going in to see if I can find quilts and blankets for us to use in the barn. If you'll get the cook stove out and anything we'll need in way of pots and pans, I'll go through the bedrooms and gather up what I can find."

Ronnie started assigning men to help with the kitchen duty while Sawyer went into the house through the back door. Although he could still smell the bodies, the stench wasn't as bad as before. He walked around the dead man and woman and wondered how they died, or if they were murdered. It was impossible to tell, based on their decomposed state.

In the first bedroom he came to, he removed all the covers from the bed and shoved them through the broken-out window.

In the second bedroom, which must have been the one the man and woman used, he was shocked at the image he saw as he faced the mirror on top of the dresser. He was troubled at his reflection. At twenty-four years old, he stood tall with broad shoulders and a narrow waist. But the brown hair that tumbled past his shoulders and the matted-up beard that hung to his chest made him look older than he was. The crow's feet at the corners of his eyes made him realize just how exhausted he really was. He looked so bad that he hardly recognized himself as he pushed his hair back with one hand so he could see his blue sunken-in eyes.

He needed a bath in the worst way, along with new clothes. His jacket had threads hanging from the elbows, and there were holes in his military issued britches.

He looked in the dresser and found a clean set of long johns and socks. He hadn't seen socks in months, and the ones he had on were nasty and full of holes. Inside the top left drawer was a .36 caliber Navy Colt in a nice civilian holster. He examined the pistol and then searched for powder and balls. This would make a nice addition to his personal arsenal.

The closet was next. Several dresses hung from rods, and on a shelf were britches and shirts. He pulled out a pair of the pants and held them up to his waist. They looked like they might fit, so he took two pairs since the owner wouldn't need them anymore. On the floor of the closet was a beautiful pair of high-top, black slip-on boots. He smiled at his good fortune.

He sat on the bed, unlaced his right boot, and pulled it off. The smell from his dirty foot was terrible, but at this point it didn't matter, as long as it wasn't as bad as the rotten corpses in the kitchen. He pulled on the riding boot, and it felt good on his foot. After getting both boots on, he backed away from the mirror far enough that he could see his new footwear. They looked wonderful, and he was proud of his first pair of riding boots.

He went ahead and threw more bed coverings out the broken window, but the new clothes he carried with him when he left. As he started out the front door this time, he was interrupted by a soldier. "Sergeant, you need to come and see what we found out behind the barn."

"Okay, let me put my things down inside the barn. What's your name, soldier?" asked Sawyer.

"Well, sir, I'm Houston Crawford. But everyone calls me Cowboy."

Sawyer looked at the young man with long blond hair and hardly any facial whiskers. He was tall and lanky and the thing that caught his attention was the cowboy boots he wore. "I can tell by your voice that you're not from Kansas, so I'm thinking you're from Texas."

"Yes sir, I was born and reared in East Texas. My pa named me Houston after the great Sam Houston."

"Look, don't call me sir. I'm a soldier just like you are. Let's go see what you found behind the barn."

Three soldiers stood in the way and moved over when Sawyer approached so he could see what they had found. He saw a hole that was four feet deep, eight foot long and three feet wide that had most likely been used as a trash burn pit for the people that lived here. Inside the hole, partially covered with trash and dirt, was an exposed hand, foot, and what was left of the top of what used to be a head.

"How many corpses do you figure are in there?" asked Sawyer.

"It's hard to tell for sure without getting in there and moving the trash out of the way, but I'm guessing there are at least a half dozen Johnny Rebs in there. I reckon we should find some shovels and finish covering them up."

Sawyer looked at the soldier. "That's up to you. I don't care and neither do they. They been dead so long that they don't even stink. I'm going back to the barn to find a washtub so I can take a bath. You men might ought to have a guard posted in the barn loft, in case we have Yankee company ride up the lane to the house." He turned and walked back to the barn. War was cruel and inhumane at times; those poor souls had been killed sometime back and there wasn't nothing he could do for them now.

Sawyer was able to find a washtub in the barn and some lye soap in the kitchen. A few men had already butchered the cow by now, and steaks were cooking in frying pans while jerky dried in the oven.

The lye soap burned his skin since he had to scrub so hard to remove the dirt and grime from his body. This was the first bath he had taken in six months or more. He thought about cutting his hair and beard but decided against it for the time being.

After he'd scrubbed off the dirt that covered his body, he got out of the tub, poured out the dirty bathwater, and refilled the tub with clean water. It was cold since he drew it straight from the well, but he wanted to soak a little longer while coming up with a plan for himself and the men. He couldn't just leave them here and go on his way. No sir, that was not like him.

He decided to stay at the farm at least four more days and give the men food and rest. Then they would load up on the horses and the wagon and head to Clarksville where their company was supposed to be. The road they were on went to Little Rock, and they would turn west there to rejoin their unit and hopefully pick up supplies for the trip.

# Chapter Twelve

By the afternoon of their third day staying at the farm, the soldiers had all taken baths and washed their filthy clothes. Some had even let their friends use a pair of horse shears to cut their hair and trim their beards. They had filled up on canned vegetables and beef meat, and the oven on the old cook stove was continuously full of dehydrating meat for jerky.

Sawyer, Ronnie, and another Texan by the name of Harold Wayne Dallas had become friends and sat in the shade of a large tree jawing about life. They had a fruit jar full of water with them and were enjoying each other's company when the lookout in the barn called out.

"Riders coming in, and they don't look friendly."

"Grab your guns and warn the others to take up defensive positions. I'm going to see who they are," said Sawyer. He pulled both his Colt Dragoon pistols and walked to the front of the house to stand inside the doorway.

Five heavily armed men rode into the yard and as

they dismounted, Sawyer called out, "Y'all can just stay where you're at or die. I've got fifteen guns aimed at you."

"Now hold on a second!" said one of the men. "We mean you no harm. We're some weary travelers looking for a little water and food."

Sawyer stepped out of the doorway with both guns pointed at the intruders. "I don't know you, and I'm not one to offer hospitality. Now shuck them hog legs or die where you are."

"Boy, we fight for General Thompson, and I don't think you want to buck us in battle. I'm Captain Buck Brown, and I'm sure you've seen what we can do. So stick your tail between your legs and run off before I shoot you for the fun of it."

Sawyer didn't appreciate the man's bad attitude and he already knew what he was going to do. "I'm so sorry, Captain, I apologize to you and your men right here in front of God and those poor souls you murdered." He took one step toward the men and the first slug hit Captain Brown in the center of his forehead, taking the back of his head off. Sawyer raised both guns to shoulder level and fired at the remaining men until both guns were empty. Then he reached behind his back and pull the Navy Colt he had found in the house and began shooting again.

A bombardment of rifle fire exploded behind him. The guerrilla fighters were shot dead, and his men came out from their positions.

"Reload your guns and get back into position, this may not be over with yet. There could be more of them close by," said Sawyer as he walked to the dead bodies to search them.

The scent of gunpowder filled the air, as well as the stench of body fluids, since some of the dead men had emptied their bowels in death. But he continued his search.

Corporal Boatwright walked over. "Sawyer, do you know who these men are?"

"Not really. They said that they were guerrilla fighters working for General Thompson, but I didn't buy that none a'tall. Why would Rebel guerrilla fighters kill their own men and put them in a gully for wild animals to eat? Come on, let's go through their pockets and see what kind of money they have on them."

Ronnie Bristow came running up to catch the horses, which were excited and snorting at the smell of blood. "These are some pretty good-looking cow ponies. They'll come in handy when we leave here tomorrow," he said while calming the animals down.

Sawyer searched through Captain Brown's pockets and pulled out a roll of Union Greenbacks. "Corporal, it's just as I suspected. These are Union soldiers, and this money proves it. I have a feeling the others may have some money on them as well."

"Yep, each of them has a little money in their pockets. What do you want to do with the bodies?"

"Drag them down to that gully where they took our soldiers and leave them there for the buzzards and coyotes."

"You don't want to bury them?"

"Corporal, I have no love for these murdering scumbags. As far as I'm concerned, being torn apart by animals is too good for them. You do what you want, but I'm not helping."

Sawyer went back to his chair under the shade tree

and reloaded his guns. Ronnie and Harold came back over and reloaded their rifles. Both men also now had on the pistols that they'd taken off the dead Union soldiers.

"Sawyer, have you gave it much thought what you're going to do when this war is over?" asked Ronnie.

Sawyer looked at his friend for a second. "I reckon I'll go back to Kansas and become a farmer. That's what my folks are, and we did all right working the ground. What're your plans?"

"I don't know if you know this, but there are thousands of Texas longhorns running wild in east and south Texas. Me and Harold are goin' to put us a crew together and gather those beasts out of the brush and mesquite thickets. It's going to be some long hard days, but we should be able to capture enough cattle to start ranching. We've been thinking that we would like for you to join up with us," said Ronnie.

"Thanks for the offer, but I don't know diddly-squat about cattle. I lived on a farm with only five milk cows and six work horses."

"You think about it anyway. When the time comes, we could all become ranchers and have more than enough money to blow," said Harold.

"Right now, the only thing I think about is keeping myself alive long enough to be able to do something else. I'm tired of these conditions and ready for this war to be over with," said Sawyer.

While they were jawing, another soldier came walking up. He was around six feet tall, with bulging muscles. He wore a mustache that came down to his chin and his hair was cut shorter than most of the others. What set him apart from everyone else was his hat—a western-style beaver felt.

"Howdy boys, I've been mulling over your offer to find them cows when this war is over and I do believe there ain't no place else for me to be, so if you still want me, I'm in."

"Heck yes, we still want you. Sawyer, this is Alton Hooter James. He goes by Hooter most of the time. He grew up herding cattle, and we asked him to join in. Hooter, this is Sawyer McCade. He's in charge around here being as he's the Sergeant and meaner than a mountain lion."

Sawyer stood up and extended his hand for Alton to shake. "Howdy, Hooter. I've been seeing you around here, but now it's nice to meet you. So your last name is James?"

"Yes sir, it's James. It's nice to meet you too, Sergeant. You're a force to be reckoned with when you draw those pistols. That was some fine work out front taking on those men. They didn't see you coming with both of them guns."

"Thanks, it seems to come easy to me. Say, Hooter, are you related to Frank and Jesse James?"

"Yeah, we're third cousins. But I ain't never seen them since we was little kids," replied Hooter.

"I met Frank and Jesse in '64, right before I came to Arkansas to scout for General Thompson. We were part of Quantrill's raiders back then. We weren't good friends since I was gone most of the time scouting out our next battle. I have to say, though, there ain't another fighting unit on either side of this war any better at killing than his raiders. I'm glad to be done with Quantrill, especially after the massacre in Lawrence. I don't want anything to do with killing women and children. The last I heard, the James boys were fighting back east somewhere."

"We all heard about what Quantrill did in Lawrence. That sure did hurt the efforts of the South. That wasn't war, it was plain murder," said Ronnie.

"I agree with you," said Hooter. "I hope my cousins weren't involved, but I'm hearing they were."

Sawyer stood up. "I think it's time to eat and then get some sleep. We've got a long, hard ride ahead of us tomorrow."

"I agree. We might as well eat and settle down for the night," said Ronnie. "At least we don't have to walk anymore since we have horses to ride. No Texas cowboy likes to walk, and we've walked our share of miles during this war."

The four men walked together to the cook stove, where two soldiers were cooking the last of the beef. With plates filled with meat and canned vegetables, they sat on the ground and dined.

Sawyer was not one to talk while he ate, so he finished his plate of food in silence and then put his plate in a washtub they'd set up for dirty dishes.

Sawyer stood up and shouted. "If I could have everyone's attention for just a minute. In the morning, I'm leaving out of here early to scout out the road going to Little Rock. Since I've got on civilian clothes, I shouldn't have any problems with Union troops. Those of you that are still not well, y'all can ride in the wagon and the rest of you ride horses. There's a couple of saddles in the tack room and the wagon is in the lean-to shed." He pointed to Corporal Boatwright. "Corporal, you make assignments for who harnesses up the wagon and who rides in it. Also assign someone to load all the food we can take in the wagon. I would suggest that everyone fills their canteen before we leave here tomorrow."

"Sergeant, what do you want to do about them bodies in the house and in that gully back there?" asked one of the soldiers.

"Nothing! Those people are dead and don't have a clue as to what's going on here. The buzzards and wild animals have to eat also," said Sawyer, unconcerned.

With that said, Sawyer went to the makeshift bed he'd made for himself in the barn. It was evening and this was his time of the day to lie awake and think about tomorrow. He didn't know where the company of soldiers he belonged to was or if they were still together. All he knew was that they were headed to Clarksville for some battle, and that information came from a Union soldier. He didn't know how long it would take them to get to Little Rock, or what kind of resistance they might encounter along the way. He shook his head; it would have been much easier if he'd kept riding after he came across these men when they had been pinned down by the river. But that wasn't the kind of man he was. He had made friends with some of them and they needed a leader to help them get back with the main company of troops. So he would stick with them until the end.

# Chapter Thirteen

Sawyer rode away from the homestead in the early morning hours while the rest of the troops made final preparations to load up and leave the farm. He didn't want to get too far ahead of them, but he didn't want to be within eyesight of them either. If trouble came their way, he wanted to be free to use his skills from the back of his horse. The past week had shown that he had a talent with his pistols. He had used a rifle during his entire service until he took the pistols off the Union officers.

He was also glad to be back in the saddle and not have to walk anymore. The few days on the back of his horse had been nice. Then he let the wounded use his animal for that one day and he grew tired of walking again that day. From now on he would ride a horse.

The sun was coming up over the horizon, and from the road, he could see a few people walking to their fields to work. Farmers, what a life they had, walking behind a team of mules all day plowing up the ground. Then going back over the same ground with a cultivator, planting seed. As the plants grew, it was an endless chore to hoe the weeds that stole nutrients and water from the desired plants. Farmers had to contend with the weather—there was either too much rain or not enough, and hailstorms destroyed crops. Then there were the grasshoppers and worms.

Maybe he didn't want to be a farmer after all. Maybe he should start having deeper conversations with his new friends about dragging those wild longhorns out of the brush and living a life of a rancher.

The first eight miles on the road traveling south went by without incident, and he had just ridden across a low-water crossing when he decided to stop to water his horse and let him rest. The small stream had plenty of places for animals to walk down the low banks and take on water. Sawyer dismounted and led his horse to drink.

He got a feeling that someone was watching him, so he reached down and drew one of his pistols and cocked the hammer back.

A coarse voice spoke from behind and to his left. "Friend, you put those hands where I can see them. I've got you dead to rights with this Sharps."

"Mister, I'm not looking for trouble. I just want to water my horse and then ride on." Sawyer gave the right shoulder of his horse a subtle nudge, moving its hindquarters to give Sawyer protection from the man's line of fire.

"You keep that hoss still, you hear? I ain't got much patience and I'll shoot you where you stand."

Sawyer gave the horse another nudge and as he moved, Sawyer brought his gun up and aimed it at a huge man with a grizzled beard dressed in hides. He pulled the trigger, hit the man in the chest, and followed it with a second and then a third slug.

The man dropped his rifle and gripped his chest, but blood kept oozing between his fingers. His eyes glazed over and his mouth opened as he tried to speak. He went to his knees and then fell face-down, dead.

Sawyer pulled his powder and lead out to reload the spent cylinders. He was getting fast at doing it since he'd had so much practice lately. He holstered the gun and walked to the man, grabbed him by his arm, and turned him over so he could go through his pockets. There wasn't much of value except two one-dollar Yankee Greenbacks. He added the two dollars to the rest of the money he had taken off dead soldiers and mounted up.

In the late afternoon, he set up his camp alongside a fast-running stream and built a fire. The stream was full of trout, and if the men had any fishing line and hooks with them, they could possibly catch enough for supper. Some soldiers carried those sorts of things in their gear, but Sawyer didn't. He did wet a hook every now and again, but it wasn't high on his list.

He went back to the road, pulled a dead tree onto the path, and made a crude arrow on the ground, hoping the troops would see it. The camp was far enough off the road that it shouldn't be seen. There was also plenty of space for the horses to graze and rest.

He lay on his bed and napped until he heard the rattling of the wagon's trace chains. Sawyer hurried to a large tree beside the creek and waited there until he could be sure it was his unit riding in. The first man he saw was Hooter sitting tall in the saddle with his rifle across his lap, ready for action.

"Hooter, don't shoot, it's me. Come on in and we'll rest here for the night."

"I figured that tree was your way of telling us where you were. I'll ride back and lead the others in. We'll be here directly," said Hooter.

The next three days went by without any altercations from Union troops, although they passed lots of folks on the road. Most people greeted them and some even answered Sawyer's questions about troop movements. Sawyer stayed closer to the wagon and men to tighten up the small convoy. One of the wounded soldiers who had been riding in the wagon bed died on the third day. When they stopped for the night, some of the men dug a shallow grave and buried him.

The next morning, Sawyer was up at daylight talking to Corporal Boatwright. "We can't be more than twenty miles from Little Rock by what information I've been getting from travelers on the road. I'll go on ahead and scout it out, and I think you should keep the men here on alert until I get back. I have a feeling in my gut that there could be bad trouble for us when we ride in. I want to check it out so we don't ride into a trap."

"Okay, I'll pass the word. Do you want someone to ride along with you into town?"

While Sawyer and Corporal Boatwright were talking, another soldier came over to them. "I overheard your conversation and had to tell you that Little Rock fell to the Yankees in '63. I was there when they came in with 15,000 troops and took over the arsenal and the state capital. We ran from there like scalded dogs. I'm thinking there's still a lot of troops stationed there."

"What's your name, soldier?" asked Sawyer.

"It's Private Douglas, sir. I'm from northwest of here."

Sawyer looked at the scrawny man with a jagged scar across his cheek. "I take it that you're familiar with the land due west of here?"

"Yep, I know most of what's out there."

"If what you say is true, then it would be suicide for us to ride into Little Rock. I want you to lead the way west and let's bypass the capital altogether. We can head toward Clarksville from here. I'll go on in and scout around and see if I can find out for sure that the main company detachment came through here on their way to Clarksville."

"Sawyer, are you sure you don't want a partner? Ronnie could go with you since he has on range clothes now," said Corporal Boatwright.

"No, I think it's best I go in as a lone civilian to make them think that I'm just riding through."

Sawyer replaced the Army saddle he'd been using with one the men had taken from the farm, so he would have no ties to the Army except the modified holsters on his hips. He thought about what Douglas had said about Little Rock falling in '63. As far as he could remember, there'd been no talk of it. With supplies being nonexistent and his detachment retreating all the time, it was hard to receive orders or updates about the war.

Sawyer knew that the war had changed him from a raw-boned farm kid to a guerrilla fighter and killer. As a scout and tracker, he had spent the majority of his time alone hiding out and surviving by any means he could acquire on his own. He often wondered what this war was really about. Men killing men, brothers killing brothers...it was absurd that people would think of doing things like that, let alone allow it to happen in reality. The memory of what that first man he'd killed in battle looked like—he'd made the mistake of looking into the dead man's eyes. That sight lingered in his mind for months, even after he had killed more men. Sawyer was finally able to push all thoughts and images from his very being and created a mental block so the things he had done didn't torment him or cause him to have remorse or even any sympathy for his victims.

He had to quit thinking those thoughts and watch the road as he rode into Little Rock. Once in town, Union soldiers were everywhere. They walked along the boardwalks and crossed the streets as he rode by. Sawyer pulled up to the first saloon he came to and went inside. About three-quarters of the patrons were Union soldiers playing poker, drinking, and talking to the girls that waited tables and flirted with the customers. Sawyer went to the counter and when the barkeep came over, he said, "I'd like a cool beer if you've got one."

"Coming right up," said the bartender. He returned in a few seconds and set the mug on the counter with foam running down the side of the glass. "That'll be four bits. Are you passing through or staying a while?"

"Passing through on my way back to Texas," said Sawyer as he drank half his beer.

The barkeep leaned over the counter. "I'd advise you to finish up and get out of here. Those holsters are a dead giveaway that they came off a Yankee officer."

Sawyer gulped down the last of the liquid and turned toward the door. He was almost out on the boardwalk when someone called out to him. "Hey cowboy, hold it right there."

Sawyer turned around with his right hand on his gun. "Soldier, you be really careful with what you're about to say. I'm not in a good mood today."

"I see you have on Union holsters and guns. We want to know where you got them."

"You're not at a rank to question me and it's none of your business, but I happen to freelance for Major General Price up in Missouri. Now sit down and enjoy your drink, or I may have to talk to your commanding officer."

The man looked from side to side at the rest of the room to see if anyone was going to back him up before he sat back down.

Sawyer walked out of the saloon and mounted up. He was ready to get out of there, although he had one more stop before leaving. He went into a gun shop and purchased two holsters that fit the Colt Dragoons. That had been a close call, and if those men hadn't backed down, he'd now be dead because of those Yankee holsters.

A small trading post sat on the banks of the Arkansas River, at the west edge of town. Downstream a couple of hundred yards was a ferry that would take him across the river.

He went inside the trading post and stood looking around before saying anything. "I'd like two large coffee pots and ten pounds of coffee, it you have that much," he finally said to the shopkeeper.

"Yes sir, I have that much and plenty more. I reckon you want those pots in a potato sack so no one will know what you've got?"

"Yeah, that's a good idea. Is there a checkpoint down by the ferry?"

"Yep, there is. But if you ride north for about ten miles, there is another ferry that you and your men can use. I'd stay clear of Little Rock as much as possible. There's something big going on with all the Yanks coming into town lately."

"Do you happen to know anything about a Rebel detachment passing by in the last week or so, heading west?" asked Sawyer as he lay some money on the counter.

The man pushed the money back to Sawyer. "Yeah. They passed by, but not without casualties. They made the mistake of getting too close to town and got waylaid by Union troops. I don't know how much you know about this war in other parts of the country, but the rumor is that General Lee has surrendered to General Grant and the war's over. I suspect we'll all hear about it in a week or so. In the meantime, I recommend you and your men use the ferry north of here and ride west. If the war is really over, then they will want you to lay down your arms somewhere and I wouldn't do it here."

Sawyer picked up his sack. "Thanks for the coffee and pots. I appreciate the information." He started toward the door.

"Iffin' I was going toward Fort Smith," said the man. "I'd travel along the north side of the river as much as possible. Fort Smith is northwest of here and if you go up to Faulkner County, you can follow the river through Pope County and stop at Cactus Flats and Ozark for supplies. There's roads that you can travel once you get into Faulkner County that should be safe for your men. That way you don't have to cross back and forth across the Arkansas River, and you should be able to find shelter from people that still love the South."

Sawyer nodded at the man. "Thanks again for your kind hospitality." And he continued to his horse. He tied his sack onto the saddle and headed upstream, hoping to find his men before they crossed the river. He didn't tell the man that they were going to Clarksville and not Fort Smith; it was none of his business. The ten miles seemed more like fifteen because of all the swamps and low-lying fields he had to skirt. In the late afternoon, he came across wagon tracks and urged his horse to go faster. Sure enough, he caught up with his men, who were also going in the direction of Faulkner County.

"Howdy, men. Did you encounter any trouble along the way?" asked Sawyer.

"No, but we did talk to some folks that saw more of our men going in this direction. I suppose they're following the river to Clarksville," said Ronnie from atop his horse.

"Well, it's a good thing that we didn't ride into Little Rock. The Union army is everywhere in town, and I was told that there are 15,000 troops around there. The man at the trading post told me that some of our men came this way and that we should stay on the north side of the Arkansas River all the way to Fort Smith. He didn't know we're only going to Clarksville. We can get supplies in Faulkner and Pope County. The folks there are sympathetic to the South. And we can also stop at a town called Ozark."

"Ozark is past Clarksville, so we won't be stopping there unless we go to Fort Smith. We need to get as far from Little Rock as we can today," said Corporal

71

Boatwright. "There is no way we want to go against that kind of odds."

"I agree with you, so let's get going and try to put some distance between us and the Yanks. I'll ride on ahead and find us a good campsite for the night. By the way, I bought us some coffee back at a trading post."

"That's the best news I've heard in a while, and I know the men will be tickled to have some java for a spell."

# Chapter Fourteen

The weary soldiers finished their evening meal and sat around the dying campfire sipping strong coffee and talking.

Sawyer called out, "I'd like for everyone to get in close so I don't have to talk loudly. When I was visiting with the man at the trading post today, he said he suspects something big is happening, and that's one reason there're so many troops at Little Rock. He heard through the grapevine that General Lee has surrendered to General Grant and that the war is over. Although he also said there hasn't been any official announcements from the Union General in charge at Little Rock."

The men sat with cups halfway to their mouths, frozen with surprise. Sawyer could tell by their lack of words and by their expressions that they didn't know what to say or how to act with that news. Finally Sawyer said, "We're going to continue with our plan until someone comes and tells us different. If the war is

73

over, I'm sure we'll hear about it and I'm also sure the Yanks will want us to lay down our guns."

"I ain't giving them my gun," said one of the men.

Another man said, "It'll be over my dead body before I give up my gun to a Yankee to be shot in the back."

Sawyer put both hands in the air to get their attention. "Hold on, I said that they'll probably want you to lay down your guns. I didn't say you had to. I, for one, will just ride back to Kansas and call it quits."

"I hope the rumor is true. I've got wild cows to wrangle and a ranch to build," said Ronnie, smiling.

The soldiers spent another hour talking about family and what they hoped to do once they were home.

The next morning, they broke camp to continue their quest for Clarksville, Arkansas. They traveled without incident and that afternoon they rode into Cactus Flats and stopped at Shinn's Store, where they bought provisions. Potatoes and bread went a long way toward feeding fourteen men. Then they rode on, hoping to get a few more miles in before dark since the days were beginning to get longer.

The small band of troops spent the next four days traveling toward Clarksville. Sawyer rode point about a mile in front of everyone else, and if they needed to get off the road, he would let them know.

On the fifth day they left the trading post in Pope County, where they had stopped long enough to load the wagon with more provisions. They were crossing little Piney Creek when Sawyer, who had already crossed, turned upstream looking for a campsite for the night. He came around a bend in the stream to find an encampment of Confederate soldiers. Four soldiers came toward him with their rifles aimed at him. He put up both his hands and said, "I'm Sergeant Sawyer McCade and I'm looking for my company. Who's in charge here?"

"That would be Captain Stevenson. You come on along and don't try anything, or we'll have to kill you," said a young private.

"Lead the way. I know Captain Stevenson," said Sawyer.

The soldiers kept their rifles pointed at him as he rode in and approached Captain Earnest Stevenson, standing with a crutch under his left arm in front of one of the few tents.

"Howdy Captain, it's me, Sawyer McCade. I've been trying to catch up with you for days. I've got thirteen more men with me coming this way."

"Sergeant McCade, I'm delighted to see you. I thought you were killed in that skirmish west of Chalk's Bluff."

"I must have got hit in the back of my head and missed the battle. I finally woke up and there were dead soldiers everywhere, so I put together some weapons and started out to find you all. I ran into these other soldiers back on the Current River and they tagged along."

"When we attacked west of Chalks Bluff, the Bluecoats came at us hard. We had to retreat and head south, only to encounter more resistance outside of Little Rock. Our casualties were high—that place was crawling with Yankee soldiers and they jumped us north of town. We've been here for two days trying to build up our strength."

"Have you received any orders or news about the war?" asked Sawyer.

"I sent a runner to General Thompson in Chalk's Bluff for orders on where we're to go next. I suspect we'll get a reply soon," said Captain Stevenson.

"I heard that General Lee surrendered to General Grant and that the war is over. Have you heard anything about that?" asked Sawyer.

"No, I haven't. But it doesn't surprise me one bit. We've been losing every battle and our supply lines are nonexistent anymore," said the captain. "Do your men have any supplies with them? We're almost out of food and our powder and lead are all but gone."

"We stocked up on flour, potatoes, and coffee at the trading post in Pope County earlier today. I'm going to ride back and get the men and bring them here," said Sawyer.

The group of soldiers had made it across the creek with the wagon loaded with food and injured men when Sawyer caught back up with them. He stopped them to make an announcement. "Men, my detachment is north of here about a mile. They're camped in a field close to the river. They've taken a lot of casualties since I last saw them, and I suspect there are less than sixty men in all. We're going to go on in and set up camp with them and start cooking some of those potatoes and make skillet bread. Corporal, I want you in charge of the food. Ration it out—one plate per man. We only have enough for maybe two days."

"Yes sir, I can do that. Do you suppose we can go back to the trading post and buy more food tomorrow?" asked the corporal.

"If need be. We're going to play this by ear for a few

days. The captain has sent a runner to General Thompson, and word is expected back any day now. If the war is over, then our Confederate money will be useless, and we only have a little Union money that we took off those troops a few days back, which means we'll have to pay for any food with Union Greenbacks. For now, let's go get settled in and maybe I can get the captain to send out hunting parties to kill us some fresh meat."

The men rode into camp and set up their own little area. They started two cook fires, and some of the injured men peeled potatoes and onions and put them in pots of boiling water. Others walked around trying to find friends and acquaintances, but to no avail. The detachment had lost a lot of men, and they didn't recognize any of the soldiers that were there.

Sawyer went to Captain Stevenson's tent to have a conversation concerning food for the men. He didn't want to spend the Greenbacks that he'd taken off the Union soldiers to feed the entire detachment.

"Captain, I recommend that you send out hunting parties to kill us some fresh meat."

"I think that's an excellent idea, Sergeant McCade. I'm putting you in charge of that assignment."

"Excuse me, but I wasn't volunteering to take this on. I think me and my men have done plenty to supply food for your troops already."

The captain pointed his finger at Sawyer. "Sergeant, I'm still in charge and you'll obey my orders as long as I'm in command."

Sawyer didn't like those orders but did as he was told. "Yes sir, I'll find some men and they can get started." Sawyer left the captain's tent and found a group of soldiers as they sat on logs and talked. "I need volunteers that are good hunters to go on a hunting mission for fresh meat."

The men sat staring at him, and not a single one volunteered. "So, no one wants to hunt for food to eat?" asked Sawyer. Still, no one said anything. "In that case, you get none of the food we have cooking on our fires, and if you try to get a plate, I'll shoot you where you stand."

Livid, he turned to leave.

"Sergeant, I can hunt but I ain't got no powder or balls for my gun," said one of the soldiers.

Sawyer turned back. "I can get you enough ammunition to kill us some food. Come with me."

Sawyer had a total of ten men volunteer to go off to hunt. They were each given some ammo, and he broke them up into five teams along with one of the horses per team to carry the meat back on. The troops could hear a shot every so often for the rest of the afternoon and early evening.

The men in camp cut limbs from trees and set up gin poles to hang the deer to skin and process the meat.

It was after dark when the last hunting party arrived back with their kill. The troops had already skinned out seven deer and two turkeys, and the last party brought in a wild hog. Some of the men stayed up until after midnight processing the animals.

The next morning, Sawyer's men were once again building up their fires and digging pits alongside them. They lay hot coals in the pits, put the deer on top of hot embers, and covered them with more coals. The animals would cook fast that way, and the meat would be tender.

A few of the men took the hog and laid it over the

coals on one of the fires. Every so often they would slide sticks under it and turn it over for even cooking. Sawyer was relieved that they had enough food for a couple more days. He had other plans for his money.

Around noon the following day, a rider came from the north and the men got to their feet, expecting to receive marching orders to another location. Captain Stevenson hadn't passed on the rumor that Sawyer had told him about the war being over, but everyone knew it since they talked to the men that came with Sawyer.

The rider stopped his lathered horse. "Someone go get the captain. I've got some important news."

"Here I am, soldier, give me the message," said Captain Stevenson as he came out of his tent pulling up his suspenders.

The soldier handed papers to the captain, who silently read them. When he finished, he hollered out and pulled his pistol and fired one shot into the air so he had everyone's attention.

"Men, I've got orders from General Thompson. They read as follows: 'The war is officially over. General Lee surrendered to General Grant on April 9, 1865. I surrendered the Arkansas Command on May 11, 1865. Men, it's been an honor to lead you in our endeavors, but now it's time to move on with our lives. You can go to Fort Smith and lay down your arms and receive your pardons for fighting against the United States. God Bless.'"

The troops whooped and hollered. Some danced around while others stood stunned with tears of joy rolling down their cheeks.

"Captain Stevenson, I won't be riding to Fort Smith to lay down my guns. In the morning, I'm leaving for

Kansas to see my folks and put this war behind me," said Sawyer.

"Sergeant, you can go, but that horse you're riding stays here with us to use. It's property of the Army and we need it. You can take enough food for two days, but that's all. Is that understood?"

"No, sir! There's no longer an Army and you're no longer in command. That horse is mine, and I'm taking him with me, along with all the coffee and some of the food I bought out of my own money. If you try to stop me, then you'll be the first one to die. I think it's a crying shame that the war has been over for almost a month, and no one had the decency to let us know until today."

Sawyer knew the defeated, crippled captain was no match for him and would do the same thing he'd done with Yankee soldiers lately when a battle started—cave under pressure.

"Okay, you're free to take your horse and what grub you'll need. The ones that want to follow me can do so and be pardoned in Fort Smith. I hope there're no hard feelings between us over this incident."

"Nope, none on my part." Sawyer stuck out his hand. "I'll go ahead and say my goodbyes now, if you don't mind."

They shook hands and Sawyer went to his bed and sat down to join in the conversation with the Texas cowboys who had set up in the same spot.

"I'm heading on to Kansas at first light. I suggest you boys do the same and head for Texas. Take you enough food for a few days. I'm rustling up my provisions tonight and if you want that second coffee pot to take with you, it's yours."

"I sure wish you would come with us," said Ronnie.

"Yeah, we could use a hard worker like yourself," said Hooter.

"I've been gone from home for three years, and it's time I get back to see my folks and my sister. If I get a hankering to join up, where might I find you?"

"You ride to Clarksville, Texas, and we'll leave word at the saloon where we can be found."

"Fair enough," said Sawyer as he got up and went to the wagon and gathered supplies that he could take with him. He went ahead and gave his friends half the coffee along with the second pot. He took jerky, potatoes, flour, salt, and coffee to start the trip home.

# Chapter Fifteen

The tall, young fighter walked his horse through the dead soldiers scattered over the small clearing overlooking the Arkansas River. He had never been to Fort Smith before, but looked forward to riding past it and into Indian Territory. He had heard stories about the Territory and how outlaws, thieves, murderers, and rapists went there to get away from the law. The road he was traveling was within eyesight of the north side of the river all the way to Van Buren, Arkansas, where he stopped at the mercantile store for supplies. He bought a couple of ground tarps and blankets, along with socks, another change of clothes, and rain gear.

When he left the store, the wooden sign outside the hotel got his attention, as well as the small café between him and the hotel. One night in a fine bed and some good food wouldn't hurt, so he went to the hotel and checked in.

The hotel had a small stable out back where he boarded his horse. The food in the café hit the spot, and he ate like a man who had been on the trail for a long time. His eating etiquette was lacking to say the least, but he didn't care as he shoveled food in his mouth and let some of it drop into his beard. If he had been at his parents' back in Kansas eating like that, his ma would have leaned over the table and slapped the side of his head and told him to use his manners or leave the table. That was another thing the war had done to him; he had no manners left at all.

When he arrived back at the hotel, the man at the desk said, "Sir, if you are of a mind to take a hot bath, I have one ready in room six at the end of the hall. It's only one dollar."

Sawyer flipped the man a dollar. "I'll go get my things and be right back."

Carrying his new clothes under his arm, he went into the room to find a steaming tub of hot water waiting on him. He sat one of his pistols on a chair beside the tub and lay in the water soaking off the dirt and grime before using the scented lye soap. It was the best bath he'd had in years. Although the one at the farm was good, it couldn't compare with hot water that soothed a man's muscles.

Thoughts of the future were on his mind now that the war was over. The first thing he needed to do was retrain himself from killing people. He had been trained to not think about or care anything for the men he killed. The last three years he'd had no conscience and now that he was a civilian again, he had to live by the law of the land, and not by the law of battle. He knew he had to make better decisions than simply pulling a gun and firing.

His ma and pa were good, God-fearing folks who went to church every Sunday. They made sure that he and his sister, Nancy Lou, were raised by the principles in the Bible. He had tried to use those principles early on in the Army, but it hadn't worked. Maybe it was time to have a talk with God and ask for forgiveness and seek His face.

Sawyer finished his bath and went to his room to get some rest. He got into bed and let his tears flow as he asked God to forgive him for the things that he had done during the last three years.

That next morning, he ate breakfast at the café and then headed into Indian Territory. He wasn't sure where he was going, but he knew that home was to the northwest. Cutting across country slowed him down because the terrain was rocky with gullies and rivers. He sometimes had to ride out of the way and change direction to get around obstacles before he could cross. It took him five days to get to Tahlequah, capital of the Cherokee Indians. He spent the night and continued the next day toward a settlement that the Creek Indians had named Tulasi. There he restocked his provisions and decided to use roads to get the rest of the way into Kansas, which was now almost due north.

The eighth day after entering Indian Territory, he was riding across the plains south of the Kansas border. Most of the people he encountered were Osage Indians, plus a few white settlers.

He rode up to MacMasters Trading Post, dismounted, and went inside.

"Howdy, young feller," said the man behind the plank counter. "I have some buckets of cool chalk out back, and a pot of venison stew on the stove iffin' you're hungry."

"I'll have some of both, and then I'll need some supplies also," said Sawyer.

"You take a load off, and I'll go fetch your food and that chalk. Just have a seat."

Sawyer watched the man go into the back room and return with a big bowl of stew and a piece of cornbread. He set it on the table that some of his customers used when they stopped by to eat or drink shine.

"You eat up while it's hot. I'll go get your drink now."

Sawyer began to eat, but as soon as the man went through the back door, Sawyer followed and watched the trading post operator stand by the well and wave his hat in the air. He was setting Sawyer up to be robbed or killed. Maybe Sawyer would have a little surprise waiting for whoever came through the door. Or maybe he'd just leave a different way than he came in, in case they tried to find him on the trail.

The man came back into the small store with a half-gallon bucket of chalk and sat it on the table, and Sawyer told him what provisions he would need.

Sawyer finished his food and got up to pay for his necessities. He carried the sack in his left hand and pulled his right-hand gun before going out the door. When he reached his horse, three men rode out of the trees that were about fifty feet from the log store building and came toward him. Sawyer kept the gun hidden in his hand since he didn't want to see it when they pulled up. The element of surprise was always the best offense when in battle. He waited until they dismounted, brought the gun up and began to fire. Two of the men were on the ground by the time the third man pulled his gun, but he missed his aim and the slug hit the store building. Sawyer dropped his empty Colt, pulled his second gun out and killed the third man before he could get off another shot.

The young ex-soldier picked his empty pistol off the ground, put it in its holster and went to each man and pulled Yankee Greenbacks from their pockets. He went back inside the store to find the owner still behind the counter. Three buckets of chalk sat ready for his recently arrived guests.

"Those men won't be doing any drinking today. You should take more care when you pick who you want to rob. Now, fork over the money in that strongbox you got back there. I don't much cotton to people that try to harm me."

"Mister, I swear I didn't know those men were coming here to rob you."

"Shut your mouth and hand over the money," said Sawyer as he cocked the hammer on the gun pointed at the man. "I saw you wave your hat for them to come in. Now get the money, or you'll wind up like them."

The man handed over the box and when Sawyer opened it, there was a total of eighteen dollars and a few coins in it. He backed to the door, mounted up, and left.

# Chapter Sixteen

The rain gear that he bought in Van Buren, Arkansas, came in handy during the night when a storm blew in. When it started to rain, he used a small tarpaulin and his slicker to cover himself and slept leaning against a tree. The area where he had stopped for the night was a small clearing surrounded by trees. A wet creek was nearby where he could get water for his horse and himself. The trees protected him from the north wind that seemed to always blow in late spring.

The rain descended from the clouds steadily for almost an hour before the thunder jolted him awake and the lightning flashed across the sky. His horse got fidgety and danced around in the small clearing where he was ground staked, scared of the bright lightning bolts as they exploded within a quarter mile of their location. A few were so close that Sawyer could feel the static in the air, and he knew he needed to get away from the tree. He intended to saddle his horse and was talking to him, trying to calm him down, when a streak of lightning came flashing from the sky and struck a tree no more than a thousand feet away.

The tree lit up for a few seconds, and branches flew through the air as his horse reared up and pulled the reins from his hand. The horse turned and took off in the opposite direction from the burning tree, and Sawyer was left standing in the rain watching him run off.

He found a spot in between some old blown tree trunks where he could lean back, and covered up again with his tarpaulin and slicker. The storm finally moved out around nine in the morning, and he was able to hang up his bedding to dry out while he went looking for his horse.

Every once in a while, he would see a horse print in the soft, muddy soil. Even though it was still cloudy with only a gleam of sunlight occasionally, the air was heavy with moisture and his shirt was soaked with sweat. As he kept walking, the timber thinned out and he entered a small clearing covered in tall, green grass. There was his horse, breaking off clumps of the turf with its teeth. Sawyer talked to the animal, walked up to it and took hold of the bridle. He rubbed the animal behind its ears and mounted up bareback to go get his things back at his campsite.

The bedding was still too damp to pack up when he returned, so he decided to stay longer and make coffee and cook something to eat. By the time he had eaten and cleaned up, the bedding was dry enough to roll up and continue on toward Kansas. He would stop earlier that night and let his things dry a little more, if need be.

Sawyer got on a road that headed in a northerly direction, and urged his horse to go faster and put more miles behind them. If all went well, he would be in Kansas by tomorrow night or the day after that.

It would be good to see his family again after all his time away. He never figured that he would spend so much time fighting in other states instead of the one he lived in. His folks had tried to talk him out of going off to war, and especially joining up with the South. Where he lived, just south of Humboldt, Kansas, most people were of German descent and hardly anyone used slave labor on their farms. In fact, most folks were for the North. To the south of Kansas in the Indian Territory were the Cherokee, Chickasaw, and Choctaw nations, and they had slaves. To the east was Missouri, which was a Confederate state, and of course they had slaves.

His family owned six hundred and forty acres along the Neosho River but only farmed about half of it because of all the trees that took up land along the river. His pa worked hard every day trying to maintain the crops in the fields, plus the large garden that they planted each year to help put food on the table. During the winter months his pa, along with Sawyer, spent their time clearing out trees and tilling more ground so they could grow more crops.

The Arkansas River was to his west now that he had turned almost due north, and he traveled along a wagon road that would take him into Kansas. He remembered that there were a few trading posts along the Verdigris River; one in particular was a day's ride from his family farm.

It took another two days before he started to see fields of wheat stalks bending in the wind. Their heads were still green and not ready for harvest, but it wouldn't be long before the families that worked the farms were out harvesting the plants. Corn hadn't been planted too long ago since it was only waist high, so that meant it would be harvested in a month to six to eight weeks.

The sun sank low in the western sky, illuminating the clouds with a beautiful orange glow. Sawyer found a place where he could ford the Verdigris River and hopefully not get soaked. As he urged the horse into the water, he pulled his legs free of the stirrups and tried his best to keep his boots out of the water. It so happened that he was able to get across, since the water was only belly-deep on his horse.

Now that he was within a day's journey from home, he would push on until almost dark before bedding down. He was anxious to see his ma, pa and sister. The days on the trail had given him time to reflect on his future and how he would work on the poor attitude and sense of carelessness he'd developed while fighting the war. He had been cultivated by his superiors to kill and not think twice about it. Now that he was a civilian again, he needed to put that training behind him and learn to be a God-fearing man like his pa. That would be a challenge, but with the right motivation he would retrain himself. If all went well, he would start attending Sunday church services with his folks to hear the word of God.

When it was too dark to see, it was time to stop for the night. Hopefully it would be the last time he would have to sleep on the cold, hard ground for a long time.

# Chapter Seventeen

This was his family's land, but from the road, he couldn't yet see the house and barns. Emotions of fright and uneasiness boiled up inside of Sawyer as he sat on his horse looking across a field of wheat swaying in the breeze toward where the house should be. He removed the safety off both his guns and walked his horse down the lane that led to the homestead. What had happened here, and where was everyone? He should be hearing the sound of a blacksmith hammer hit an anvil or see his ma in the garden hoeing weeds.

He rode up the lane to the house to see dark, charred, broken beams and a pile of charred lumber that once was the house he grew up in. The area where the barn had stood tall was in the same condition. He wanted to cry with sadness, to shout out in anger at the hurt he was experiencing at that moment when he was close enough to see the devastation to his home. He dismounted in front of the charred remains of the house. For the first time in a long time, he was scared and heartbroken by what he saw. Something bad had happened and based on first glance, it had happened some time ago since weeds grew in the ashes.

After tying his horse to graze, Sawyer slowly walked around the burned-down buildings looking for anything that might tell him the story of what had happened. He went to the well, lifted the lid covering the hole and looked down into the water. He didn't see any trash or debris, which was good because whatever had happened, they hadn't destroyed the well. He needed answers to what had transpired to cause the fire, and he needed to know where his parents and sister were. That was the most important thing; the house could always be rebuilt. He went to his horse, removed his canteen and took a drink of water and looked toward the north.

There was a family plot north of the house on a small knoll, so he mounted up and rode up there to see if there were any fresh graves. Alongside his grandparents' graves were two mounds of earth that hadn't been there when he'd left to fight in the war. Both graves had crude crosses, and all that was written on them was *Ma* and *Pa*. Where was his sister? Maybe she was still alive and hopefully living nearby. That thought gave him hope; he would go into town and do his best to find her. There wasn't anything he could do at the gravesite, so he went back to the burned-out buildings and began to search out away from the burned building for horse tracks, to see if anyone had been coming here. There was nothing to indicate that anyone had been here recently. By his estimation, whatever occurred had taken place more than six months earlier, and there was nothing left in the way of clues or evidence.

Sawyer headed north toward Humboldt and at the first property he came to, he rode into the yard and called out, "Hello, Mr. and Mrs. Schmidt. It's Sawyer McCade, and I mean you no harm."

The screen door opened, and a woman and man came out onto the porch. "Hello, Sawyer, come on down and sit a spell. Samantha will get you a cool glass of water."

Sawyer dismounted, walked onto the porch, and extended his hand. "Hello, Mr. Schmidt, it's been a long time."

"Yes, it has. I wouldn't have recognized you with the beard and long hair. How have you been?"

"Well, I made it through the war in one piece, but it don't look like my folks did. Can you tell me what happened over there?"

"About a year ago, some fellers from back east moved into Humboldt and started buying up all the land they could lay their hands on. Raiders came through one day and killed your folks. We buried them in your family plot. All the farmers suspected that there was a connection between the Easterners and the raiders, but we couldn't prove anything. There's been a few other incidents like this over the past several months."

Sawyer stood there trying not to overreact or show how hurt he was inside. But this didn't sound like the raiders he knew or had ridden with, although he wasn't going to tell his neighbor that he had in fact ridden with Quantrill. Raiders didn't just hit one particular small farm; they would ride into an area and destroy every farm in their path.

"I appreciate you burying my folks in the plot. Can you tell me about my sister? I'm assuming she's alive?"

"Yep, Nancy's alive. She's in town and married to a

good man by the name of Richard Straight. He works at the seed mill; they live on the east side of town in the old Cartridge house."

"Thanks for the information and the water. I best be going." He handed the glass back to the man.

"Sawyer, you be careful in town. There's a lot of folks there who are sympathetic to the Union, and we don't want any more trouble around here. They blame the Confederates for the sporadic raids on the farms and how the war has devastated our commerce and just about put all of us in the poorhouse. Most of the farms had to take out loans to survive, and that included your folks. After they were killed, the bank foreclosed on the farm. As far as I know, it still belongs to the bank," said Mr. Schmidt.

Sawyer was confused and angered by this news. He looked at Mr. Schmidt with a frown on his face. "I thought my pa had already had his place free and clear of mortgages."

"He did until the bottom dropped out of the economy because of the war. It's been hard to make ends meet these last couple of years."

"Okay. Thanks again for talking to me. I'm going to see my sister. Please don't tell anyone that I came by. I don't want my presence known just yet."

"You bet, take care."

Sawyer was mad about his folks getting killed and the bank taking their farm. He needed to get to the bottom of it, and his sister would be his first stop.

The town looked about the same as it did before he left, except for the number of men who limped along the boardwalks with walking sticks or crutches. Some of them still wore their Union army jackets and britches;

some had an arm or a leg missing. It was sad to see the townspeople in such dire circumstances because of the war.

People stopped on the boardwalk to glare at him as they tried to figure out who he was. He recognized a few people but didn't acknowledge them. There would be time for that later.

He rode straight to his sister's house. He didn't want to be seen yet, so he took his horse around to the back of the house and knocked on the kitchen door. "Nancy Lou, it's Sawyer. Are you home?"

The young housewife came running through the kitchen and threw open the screen door, jumped into her brother's arms, and hugged his neck.

"Oh Sawyer, I'm so glad to see you alive. I thought I had lost you also."

Nancy was fifteen months older than Sawyer, and they had been close growing up. She had always used the older sister excuse to try and make him mind her, but that usually went sour and they fought often.

"It's good to see you, sister. I wish the war would have been over sooner. I went by our farm and found out that Ma and Pa are dead. Can you tell me what happened out there?"

"I certainly can, but first we're going inside to sit down and have a cup of coffee. We have a lot of catching up to do."

They sat at the table sipping coffee and Sawyer answered a volley of questions from his sister about where he had been and if he had been shot. He finally reached out and took her by the hand. "It's time you tell me what happened out at the farm."

"I got married to Richard last year and we moved

into town. About a month after I left the farm, some men rode into the yard and killed Mama and Papa. Sawyer, it was terrible. They left them lying in the front yard close to the porch. It seemed that Papa had been trying to defend the place, because his shotgun was on the ground beside him. We think that Mama saw what was happening and ran out to protect Pa, and they shot her too. Then the men set fire to the house and barns and rode off. The neighbors saw the smoke and flames and went to help. They said that they had to drag the bodies away from the burning house because the fire was already causing their skin to draw up and almost burn." She stopped and picked up a dish towel to dry the tears that were running down her cheeks. Sawyer stayed composed and gave his sister a few moments before he asked, "Did anyone see who the raiders were, or hear anything about it in town?"

"No one saw anything. And that's not all—a week later the bank president, a man by the name of Nathaniel Hopson, came here to my house and served papers to me stating that Pa hadn't paid his mortgage payments and the bank was foreclosing on the property, and I only had one week to catch up with the payment in full."

Sawyer's eyes narrowed. "Who's Nathaniel Hopson? I've never heard of him before."

"He came here about three years ago from back east and bought out the bank, saloon, and rumor is a couple of other businesses."

Sawyer sat in thought. "A week seems kind of quick, since they had just been killed. Do you still have the papers he brought to you?"

"No, I was so mad that I threw them in the fire and

they burned up. We didn't have any money and we still don't. My husband works hard, but it takes all he makes for us to survive. So, the bank took Ma and Pa's land and the very next day sold it to a company that has been buying up property around here. The gossip is the bank sold the farm for thirteen dollars an acre. Most of the land around here is selling for sixteen dollars an acre. Sawyer, the townspeople think there is something going on with the bank foreclosing on land the raiders have hit. This is not the first time attackers have burned out farms in Allen County."

"Sis, that's water under the bridge now," said Sawyer and patted his sister's hand. "The farm is gone and so are Ma and Pa. I'm going to ride back into town and look around. I'll see you again in a day or so."

"Sawyer McCade is that all you're going to do? Just ride into town and look around. For your information, it's not water under the bridge. I would have thought you would want to do more than look around."

"Sis, I'm tired of killing and fighting in a war that couldn't be won. I'm going into town now and look around." He got up and walked outside to get on his horse. She followed him into the yard and watched as he got his horse to leave.

Sawyer was struggling in side, he didn't tell her the truth—it wasn't water under the bridge and he was not going to let it drop, but he didn't want her to know what he intended to do about it. He was going to protect her at all costs, she was all he had now.

"Sawyer, I'm sorry for the outburst, don't go. You can stay here with us, and I'm sure you can find work in town."

He walked back where she stood with tears in her

eyes. "No, I could bring hard feelings or trouble on you and your husband since I fought for the South. I'm thinking about going down to Texas and start ranching with some army friends. I'll be back to see you before I go."

Sawyer and his sister hugged, and he said, "Sis, I love you, and I'm really glad you're all right."

He rode into town and rented himself a room at the hotel, signing his name as Steve Smith.

# Chapter Eighteen

Sawyer rented a second-floor corner room from which he could see the street and watch the bank. Before he could decide on his next move, he'd need to mull over the information he had gotten. He sat in the quiet of his room and watched everyone who went in and out of the bank.

At ten till five that afternoon, two men dressed in cheap-looking suits and bowler hats came down the sidewalk and entered the bank. He could tell by the bulges on their hips that they were armed. In a few minutes, the same two men came out. One of them carried a satchel that looked empty by the way the sides didn't bulge out. They walked toward the stage line office. Sawyer suspected they worked for the banker and were either sending money on the stage or collecting money when the stage arrived.

At five o'clock, the teller came out the front door like he was finished for the day, but Sawyer kept watching. Over the course of ten minutes, a few people still went inside and did their business and then came out again. The stagecoach arrived at 5:25 p.m., stirring up plumes of dust as it came to a stop in front of the Butterfield stage office. The shotgun rider threw down a heavy-looking bag, and one of the cheap-suited men picked it up while the other one handed his bag to the driver. So the satchel was empty and the men were only returning it so the stage could take it back with them to the place where it originally came from, and the bag they now had was full. And he suspected it was a shipment of money for the bank since it was heavily guarded.

He continued to watch as the two men took the bag back into the bank. About ten minutes later, they came back out with a man dressed in a fancy suit who locked the front door. Sawyer made note of the time and watched where the men went. The two cheap-suited men went into the saloon, while the other man continued down the boardwalk. Sawyer was about to lose sight of him, but happened to catch a glimpse of him turn into a large, two-story building down at the corner of the street.

It was time for supper, so Sawyer went out to the street, walked down the alley, and continued on until he was able to walk behind the back of the bank building. He looked at the surrounding structures as he walked, before coming out on the next street over.

The building on the corner that he thought he'd seen the man from the bank enter had a sign on the front that read, *McMillan Land Company*.

Sawyer found a place along the boardwalk where he could lean against an awning post and pretended to look at a paper he had picked up off a chair in front of one of the other business. He was able to look the land office over and saw an outdoor stairway going up to the second floor. If he remembered correctly, this building had been a lawyer's office on the second floor and a dress shop on the bottom floor, and that was the reason the stairs were on the outside of the building. He folded the paper, put it in his back pocket and moseyed by the front of the building, trying to look inside without being noticed. He continued on by to the café that was three business on past the land office. He didn't want to talk to anyone in the café during supper, so he ate his food and listened to the conversations of the patrons eating their evening meals and got the idea they were skeptical of the banker and the land company. He kept hearing little tidbits of negative comments about them and the men they employed.

Sawyer wanted to come up with the evidence of who actually killed his parents, but that was going to be an almost impossible task since it happened so long ago. In his mind, it wasn't raiders who had killed his folks; raiders didn't target one farm and leave all the others alone. From what information he had heard from his sister and the tidbits of talk from overheard conversations, he had the assumption that they had been murdered by men who had something to do with the banker and the land company. At this point, no one could be trusted so he had to be careful who he talked to or who he would question about the banker and land man. He would have to give himself time to think about his options and decide if he wanted to stay and try to find the killers, who could be gone from Humboldt by now or go down to Texas and become a rancher.

He had come home hoping to rekindle his relationship with his folks and pick back up the life of a farmer.

Is that what he really wanted in life now that his parents were gone? It would be nice if he had someone he could talk to for answers and seek advice from. Then a thought struck him—he could go visit the Reverend Curtis Toliver. His pa always held the man in high esteem, and he was a trusted friend of the family.

Sawyer stepped upon the porch of the little white house out behind the church building and knocked on the door. It opened and there stood an elderly man dressed in pants with suspenders over his long john top. "What can I do for you, young man?"

"I'm sorry to bother you, but I need to talk. I'm Sawyer McCade."

"Sawyer, we thought you were killed in the war. Come on inside, boy."

"Sir, I don't want anyone to know that I'm here. Please keep it a secret. It could put my sister in harm's way if the wrong people knew I was back."

"I give you my word. Now, what's on your mind?"

"I'd like to know what you think happened to my folks and how the bank took our land."

"Well, some think that raiders killed your folks."

"I'm aware of what some folks think. I want to know what you think happened," said Sawyer.

The preacher sat down in a cushioned rocker, pointing to another chair. "Sit down. I think the banker and that crook at the land company wanted your family's land along with a lot of other folks' property. It seems that every time raiders hit a place, the land was foreclosed on within a few days and then sold to the land company. Of course, the raids were blamed on William Quantrill or Bloody Bill Anderson."

"I don't think Quantrill or Anderson's men were

the raiders. I was trained in guerrilla warfare, and hitting one lone farm is not how they operate. I'm beginning to see a connection to the banker and land man myself, but I have no proof. Why exactly do you think the banker and land man are involved?" asked Sawyer.

"I'm fairly sure the banker and that McMillan feller are what's known as carpetbaggers. They come in from the east with lots of money and hired guns to take what they want. I still can't believe that your pa owed any money to the bank on his farm. As long as I've known him, your family has never borrowed money from the bank to operate and I know for a fact he had a bumper crop last year. The other interesting thing is that the judge signs off on all the foreclosure papers. One has to wonder about his involvement with these men."

"So, you think they killed my folks and came up with a trumped-up mortgage so they could steal their land?"

"Yes, I do. And I think there's been others also. You be careful who you talk to concerning these activities. They've got a lot of hired guns working for them and most of them stay at the saloon, so stay clear of it."

"Yes sir, I sure will. I'm not much on drinking and saloons. Preacher, I'm not the man I was when I left to go off to war. I'm a hard man who's taken lives, and I have no remorse for what I've done. I came back here hoping I could start over, but these circumstances have put that dream in another place and I'm not certain that I want to go down that path right now. I hope I can control my feelings enough to walk away from here and start over somewhere else, I've been involved in enough killing for a lifetime and I really want to put it behind me. I'll be leaving now; it was good talking to you. Please keep quiet about me being here."

Sawyer got to the door and turned back. "Preacher, would you be kind enough to pray for me right now?"

"Certainly, my boy, come hold my hand."

After the prayer, Sawyer walked back to the hotel and lay on his bed, thinking about what he was going to do and how he would do it. About midnight, he drifted off to sleep with a plan in his mind.

He dreamed about the time when he was ten and his family had camped on the river by his house. They put out limb lines to catch catfish, and he ran up and down the bank helping his pa take the fish off the lines. Then as he pulled the fish to the bank, they transformed from fish to dead soldiers staring up at him through lifeless eyes.

Sawyer came awake and gasped for breath before he settled back into a restful sleep.

# Chapter Nineteen

Sawyer dressed and walked to a different café the next morning. It was located about a half-block between the McMillan Land Company and the bank. He hoped that he could get a glimpse of the man who owned the business as they walked by going to work, or at least overhear some talk about him from the locals eating their meals.

Most of the conversation that morning happened to be about the war ending, and of course the stories were blown out of proportion. They were jawing about how the Union had shot the Rebs that laid down their arms and how the Union was going to start rounding up the Confederate soldiers that didn't get pardoned. They went as far as to say that all the Union soldiers were going to get land allotments for their service. Sawyer finished his food and reached into his pocket to pay for his meal when the door opened and two well-dressed men came in and sat to his right. One of the men he recognized as the bank president, and he had a feeling that the other one was McMillan.

Sawyer motioned to the girl to refill his cup and pointed to the money to pay for his meal. This was his opportunity to learn more about the men by eavesdropping on their conversation. He learned that McMillan's first name was Howard, and that the banker went by Nat, or at least that was what Howard called him. It was almost impossible to hear them talk because they were so quiet, and at times each would lean toward the other to say something. With other patrons in the room talking and noise coming from the waitress as she cleaned off tables and scurried around the room refilling cups, it was hard to overhear it all.

Sawyer finished off his coffee and stood to leave when he heard one of the men say, "Excuse me, mister."

Sawyer turned toward the men's table. McMillan pointed at Sawyer with his fork. "You any good with those guns?"

"I guess that's a matter of opinion. Why do you ask?"

"I'm always in the market for a man who can take care of himself in a tight spot. Are you that man?"

"Nope, not interested," said Sawyer and again headed to the door to leave.

"Then I suggest you finish your business in town and ride on. We don't cotton to strangers around here."

Sawyer stopped. "I totally understand, and I'll be riding on this morning," said Sawyer as he once again walked up to their table so close that no one but the two men could hear him talk. "I don't cotton to threats and if trouble comes my way, you'll be the first one I kill. So I suggest you watch your tongue around me." He slowly lifted his left hand to tip his hat, and then backed toward the door. Both men watched him as he left.

Sawyer went to the hotel, gathered up his things, and saddled his horse. Before he rode out of town, he would stop and say goodbye to his sister. He took the back way to her house so people wouldn't see him at her residence.

"Brother, I love you and want you to stay here. This is your home, even though the farm is gone," said Nancy, teary-eyed.

He took hold of her hands. "I'm a trained killer and not a nice man right now. If I stay, there is no telling what I might do, and my actions could put you in harm's way. I won't do that. Plus, the town has changed with the war and most folks will probably give us a hard time when they find out I fought for the Confederate States and rode with Quantrill. The best thing for us right now is for me to let the law take care of what's going on around here and for time to heal the anger in people. I can't bring our folks back, and it's best that I leave."

"You know how I feel about you, and I want you here with me. I wish you would take some time to reconsider before you just up and leave."

"No, I'm going to Texas to gather wild longhorns and start ranching and settle down. I need to get away from here, where the memories linger about the good times we had growing up. I believe in my heart that the banker and the land company man were involved in the death our parents so they could steal their land. They tried to hire me this morning and when I turned them down, I was warned to leave town. I can't let anyone know that I was here, or it could cause you and your husband problems."

She put both arms around his neck. "You better write to me when you get settled on your ranch."

"When I get settled, I'm coming after you and your family to live with me, so don't get too comfortable here," said Sawyer, and kissed her forehead.

He mounted and rode away, thoughtful about the storm he was about to cause for the banker. He smiled. His sister had no idea what he was about to do, and that banker and land man sure didn't know what he was capable of.

Sawyer rode north, heading to the community of Iola, Kansas. He figured he could get everything he needed from there since two stores had been settled there in 1860 before the war. The most important thing about going to Iola was, no one knew who he was there. And that would be critical to his upcoming plan.

He rode into Iola at about two in the afternoon and was surprised by how much it had grown since he'd been there five years earlier. From what he could tell, there were more businesses and houses than there were in Humboldt. With nothing to eat since breakfast, he was hungry so he found a livery stable, left his horse there, and walked to the Greasy Spoon to eat.

While eating, he struck up a conversation with one of the locals sitting at the table next to him. "I'm looking for a place to stay the night and I also need a shave and haircut. Can you suggest a barber and a place to sleep?"

"There's a small hotel on the north end of town. The owners are my kin, and the accommodations are nice. The barber is between the two stores. Just be aware that he may try to talk your leg off. He also has a bathtub in the back of his shop if you want to take a hot bath."

"How about the stores? Do they have a good selection of clothes and such? I'm thinking about sprucing up some."

"Yeah, both are well stocked and are run by friendly folks."

"Much obliged for the information."

Sawyer left the café, walked to the store, and started gathering up clothes. He selected a few shirts, a pair of pants, some underwear, and two riding dusters. One was gray and the other one was black. He found a new hat that he liked and bought it too, along with bandannas and a travel bag to hold his new items. He walked to the hotel, rented himself a room, and left most of the new things in his room. He put a few items like a shirt, britches, socks in his bag and headed to the barbershop.

"Howdy, stranger. What can I do for you?" said the barber as Sawyer came through the door.

"I'd like a haircut, shave, and a hot bath," said Sawyer.

"Yes sir. Have a seat while I get your water heating and then I'll get started. It looks like you ain't seen scissors in a long while. I'll cut off the beard first and then your hair. About how much hair do you want left?"

"I'm thinking I want the sides high and maybe the top just enough to part over to the side."

"Yes sir, I call that high and tight."

It took the man about thirty minutes to cut Sawyer's hair and shave his face smooth. He handed a mirror to Sawyer, who took it and looked at the handsome man in the reflection of the glass. Brown hair, blue eyes, straight nose, and that little smile. He looked good and knew that his plan would work the way he imagined it.

"I like it. Now for that bath."

"It's ready, right back here. Follow me and I'll get you a clean towel."

Sawyer felt like a new man after he had his bath and dressed in his new clothes. He was sure that no one would recognize him now as he went back to the livery stable.

"Say, mister," said Sawyer to the stable owner, "I'd like to trade my horse for a good cow pony if you have what I need. I'm heading down to Texas to hunt wild longhorns and need a good horse with some stamina to him."

"I have a black horse that I bought off a down-on-his-luck cowboy a while back. He's a big animal and is supposed to be a heck of a cattle horse, but I'm having a problem with him wanting to bite people so no one wants to buy him. If you're interested, I'll trade straight across." The stable owner looked at Sawyer and then asked, "You say you want to trade, but I don't see your horse anywhere."

Sawyer smiled. "He's in one of your stalls. I brought him in earlier. I'm the man with the long hair and beard."

"Well, I'll be doggone! I sure didn't recognize you. I like that horse you have in there if you want to trade."

"Let me have a look at your horse," said Sawyer.

Sawyer walked into the corral and watched the horse for a few minutes. He finally went up to the big black beast, talking softly. He stood in front of him and reached up to pet him behind his ears, and the horse grabbed his hand in his mouth. He really had Sawyer's hand in his lips and kind of held on to it.

Sawyer's first reaction was to jerk his hand back but

he didn't, and the horse didn't bite down on it. He just kept it in his mouth. Sawyer took his other hand and started to pet the animal and talk to him. The horse turned his hand loose and started nodding his head up and down while he nudged against Sawyer's shoulder.

Sawyer walked to the man and stuck out his hand. "I'll take the horse, and if you have a better saddle than mine, I'll take that also."

"I have just the thing you need if you're going to cowboy in Texas. I have an almost-brand-new Mexican Vaqueros saddle that is made for cowboying. I'll trade if you give me eight dollars to boot."

"Let's have a look-see and I'll decide if that's what I want."

"Come on, it's in the tack room. I have a fancy bridle to go with it also."

Sawyer examined the saddle and bridle, shook hands with the man, and paid for his things. Everything was in place. Tomorrow he would go back to Humboldt to execute his plan.

# Chapter Twenty

The black horse took to the trail that next day with an easy gait and Sawyer loved the padded saddle he had bought. He had on his new black hat and black long riding jacket as he made the short trip back to Humboldt, where he would hole up and wait until the right time to make his play. It had been a Monday when the men at the bank had gone after the bag at the stage station. He figured that the bank only received a shipment of money once a week, and this was Wednesday.

He detoured around Humboldt so no one would see him and kept heading south until he came to the trading post along the Verdigris River, which also happened to be a stop on the stage line where they changed out the horses.

Sawyer walked into the building that served as a trading post, café and resting place for the weary travelers while the owner changed out the horses for the stage. "Howdy," he said to the owner and his wife. "I'm looking to buy a good packhorse and pack saddle. Would you have any for sale?"

"Yes, I do." The man pointed toward the back door. "The horses are right out back, and the pack saddles are on a rail inside that shed beside the corral."

Sawyer walked out the back door and stood watching the four horses that were in the pen. He picked out a spotted mustang pony and went back inside. "How much for the spotted horse and saddle?"

"I'll take sixty dollars for them if you buy your provisions from me."

"That's fair enough, but I'm not sure when I'll need the horse or the provisions. I'm heading up to Humboldt to get my money coming in on the stage, and I'm not sure when it'll arrive. I don't want to spend what I have on me until I know when the rest will arrive."

"If it's coming in on the stage, then that'll be tomorrow. The stage line brings money on Mondays and Thursdays."

"If that's the case, then I'll go ahead and buy the animal and pack saddle and give you a list of provisions that I'll need for my trip. If you'll give me a pencil and paper, I'll write down my list and then head on to Humboldt."

Sawyer wrote down his order and handed it to the man, who looked at the paper and wrote numbers beside each item. "All total, you owe me $72.12."

Sawyer counted out the money and handed it to the man. "If my money is on the stage tomorrow, then I'll be back to get my property. But if it's late, then I'll make other arrangements with Nat the banker and come back the next day."

"That'll be fine. I'll have your things sacked up so it'll be easy to load on the packhorse."

The men shook hands and Sawyer rode north back to Humboldt. He had to admit that he had played his part with the man superbly. He now knew when the stage would deliver more money to the bank, and he had a packhorse and provisions waiting on him and no one knew what he was up to. When he was out of sight from the trading post, he spurred the horse into a run and let him open up and cover the remaining few miles. He wanted to get back to his room and watch the street again that evening.

The hotel clerk didn't recognize him and thought he was a stranger riding through. Sawyer said to him, "If the second-floor corner room is available, I'd like that one."

"Yes sir, it's available. Have you stayed in it before?"

"Yes, a long time ago. But I remember that with the windows open, you get a good breeze through that room."

"Yes sir, you do. We also have a stall out back for your horse."

"Thanks, but he's at the livery stable."

Once inside the room, Sawyer moved the chair to the window and watched the bank. At five, the teller came outside and walked down the street, prompting Sawyer to get up and go downstairs, cross the street, and walk south along the boardwalk. He took notice of the space between the bank and the buildings on either side. He stood in front of the bank and looked in the front window, spying some men sitting in an office toward the back of the lobby. He took hold of the doorknob and turned it; it was still unlocked, but he didn't open the door. He was only wanting to know if Nat locked it after the bank clerk left for the day.

It was time to continue on and not bring attention to himself, so he walked to the corner of the street and headed down the alley behind the bank. He wanted to be sure that he remembered how everything was laid out.

When he came out of the alley, he walked back across the street toward the hotel and continued to walk until he found a place to have his evening meal.

Later that night he sat at the window and went over his plan. Everything was in place, and all he had to do was wait until tomorrow afternoon.

Sawyer stayed in his room until two in the afternoon. He didn't want to be seen around town, and besides, he had gone much longer than that without eating so he was used to waiting to eat. When he came down from his room, he carried his belongings in his travel bag with him to the livery stable where he transferred his things to two saddlebags and a flour sack. He would need his clothing bag for later in the day and needed it empty.

"I'm going down to the café to get something to eat. Can you have my horse ready to go by the time I get back?" asked Sawyer.

"I sure can. I'll have him tied inside one of the stalls for you," said the owner.

"Thanks," said Sawyer, and handed the man two dollars to pay for the stall and feed.

When he came back for his horse, he tied on the flour sack, hung the bags over the saddle horn, and put on his long black riding duster. "Mister, it's been good knowing you. I'll see you around sometime."

"Sure thing," said the man.

Sawyer rode south out of town, circled around, and

came in at the back of a little shack out behind the ladies' clothing store on the south side of the bank. He tied his horse out of sight, removed the black duster, and put on the gray one. He lay the black duster over his saddle for later.

Sawyer found a shade tree where he could stay cool out of sight and hear the stage when it entered town from the south. It was a short wait, no more than thirty minutes until he heard horse hooves pounding the road. The stage came down the street, so he got up and eased between the bank and the store building next door, then removed his hat long enough to peer around the corner and see the banker's two men come walking back from the stage office with the bag of money. He also saw the teller leave the bank and head north up the boardwalk to go home for the day.

Sawyer took a couple of steps back so his shadow wouldn't show in the street and waited until he heard the door to the bank close. He counted to thirty and then came out from between the buildings and went to the door. He pulled his bandanna up over his nose, pushed the door open as easy as he could and went inside.

The men were once again in the office and as Sawyer shut the door, he turned the lock and pulled both of his guns. He had taken about three steps toward the open office door when Nathaniel Hopson looked up and his mouth opened to say something. Sawyer took two quick paces, hit one of the men in the back of the head with the gun butt and put the barrel of his other gun to the other man's chest as he stood up.

"Sit back down and keep your mouth shut," said Sawyer to the henchman.

When the man sat in the chair, Sawyer hit him in the back of his head with the butt of his gun, and he tumbled to the floor.

"Now listen, mister, you're making a big mistake coming in here this way," said Nathaniel as he looked at the masked man.

"Shut up and listen to me. You have people murdered, then you take their land and sell it to McMillan. All that comes to a halt today. I'm here to relieve you of your blood money and if you give me any trouble, I'll make an example out of you in front of the entire town."

"Do you have any idea how many men we have on our payroll that'll come after you and hunt you down, you lowlife cowpuncher?" said Nathaniel.

Sawyer pulled the Arkansas toothpick out of its scabbard, walked to the man, and pulled the blade across his throat just enough to make it bleed, causing blood to run down his shirt. The man's eyes got big and he opened his mouth.

"Don't say a word unless it's to tell me where the money bag is located," said Sawyer as he stood with the knife pointed at the bleeding man.

Nathaniel pointed to a door against the far wall, then put both of his hands to his throat to stop the flow of blood.

Sawyer grabbed hold of the handle, but the door was locked. He went to Nathaniel, who was still trying to hold back the leakage of blood, and pulled the knife back out to place it lightly against the side of his neck. "Where's the key that opens the door?" he asked as he grabbed one of the man's hands and pulled it away from his neck. Nathaniel reached into his jacket pocket, pulled out a key and handed it to Sawyer.

Sawyer opened the door, which was a heavy, three-inch wood door made to withstand a lot of force. Inside the room was the money bag. Sawyer emptied it into his travel bag and then he took stacks of bills off the shelves that lined the walls. When he finished, the bag was bulging and the shelves were empty.

The banker was sitting in his chair, white as a sheet and still clutching his throat even though it was hardly bleeding anymore since the cut was only superficial.

Sawyer sat the bag stuffed with money on Nathaniel's desk, went to one of the men he had knocked out, and felt in his pocket. He pulled out a handkerchief and walked to the scared banker. "Move your hands and I'll tie this around your neck to stop the bleeding," said Sawyer.

The banker removed his hands and let his assailant tie the cloth around his neck. It was only bleeding a tiny bit now and looked much worse than it was. Sawyer finished putting the handkerchief on, then hit the banker in the back of his head, knocking him out as well.

He pulled open the desk drawer and found paper and a pencil.

*This is our town, and we don't like murderers and thieves. This is what will happen to anyone who tries to take our land and kill our people.*

Sawyer picked up his bag, walked to the back door, looked both ways and then went to his horse. Behind a tree, he changed back into the black jacket and rode to the edge of town, where he removed three thousand dollars from the bag and put it in his pocket. He rode to Pastor Toliver's house and knocked on the door.

"Sawyer, is everything all right?" asked the preacher when he opened the door.

"Yes sir. But I'm leaving town and need a favor from you." Sawyer handed him the money. "Will you make sure that my sister gets this? I can't go to her house, it might cause her trouble."

"Don't worry, I'll see that she gets it. Can we pray before you go?"

"I'd like that, preacher."

Sawyer rode south feeling good about how things went at the bank. He could have killed the three men and never thought about it again, but that wasn't who he wanted to be anymore. It wasn't robbery that he committed at the bank, but payment from the sale of his family farm.

# Chapter Twenty-One

Sawyer pressed the black horse to run as much as possible until they were within a mile of the trading post. He wanted to get his packhorse and supplies as quickly as possible and ride on south across the Verdigris River, even if he had to do it after dark. Since he had crossed it a few days ago, he knew where he could ford the stream without getting his provisions wet. He could always make camp later in the night, given that he had been through that part of Kansas only a few days back and was familiar with the lay of the land.

The horse and supplies were waiting on him when he arrived at the trading post right after sundown. He loaded the sacks of provisions and had a quick meal before leaving. He still had an hour or more of daylight left, and the farther he could go would help him in case the banker sent his men looking for him.

Sawyer made camp about twenty-five miles north of Mr. Coffee's Trading Post, close to the border of Kansas and Indian Territory. Mr. Coffee was from Humboldt, and Sawyer's pa used to sell him grain to trade to the

Osage Indians that lived in the southeastern part of the state.

The sun's red glow peeked through the morning darkness while he saddled up his horses and headed on toward the trading post. That was where he would have his morning coffee and maybe breakfast.

The ride to the post took him longer than he expected since he had the packhorse to deal with. By the time he arrived, all he wanted was a quick meal and then to be on his way again. The quicker he got out of Kansas, the better.

He didn't know the man and woman who were tending to the trading post for Mr. Coffee. From the conversation he had with them while he ate his meal, he learned that Mr. Coffee owned three trading posts—two in Kansas and one in Indian Territory.

They informed Sawyer that the border with Indian Territory happened to be two miles away, and he would have to ride through the Osage and Pawnee Indian Reservations to continue south. They told him that the Indians were friendly, and he wouldn't have any trouble from them. And if someone came asking, they or the Indians wouldn't tell that they saw him ride through.

Sawyer covered the plains and rolling hills with ease and skirted around any settlements or houses he came across. He rode south across the grassy plains and around dusk on the third day, he heard a noise to his right. It sounded like thousands of hooves hitting the ground from over the hill to his right. It wasn't long until he saw a huge cloud of dust and the noise grew louder. The dust cloud was coming his way, and that concerned him since he didn't know what was happening.

A clump of trees that covered about three acres stood tall on the next hill to his left and up ahead about a quarter of a mile away. He spurred his horse and jerked on the lead rope of the packhorse until both were running toward the cover on the hill. He looked back to where he had ridden across the plains as he entered the trees and saw a herd of buffalo as they crested the hill he'd just come down. The ground shook from the hooves of the running beasts as they passed by where he sat on his horse surrounded by trees. Sawyer had never seen that many buffalo together in one herd before, and it was an amazing sight to watch them run by. He sat in awe of the massive buffalo as they ran, nodding their horned heads up and down. He could have been trampled to death if he hadn't taken shelter in the trees away from the animals.

Now that they were almost past his location, it looked like they were turning back toward the west. The dust cloud that was following them drifted into the trees where he sat, and it became so thick that he had to pull his bandanna up to keep the dust out of his nose and throat. He bent his head down to try and shield his eyes from the tiny particles in the air.

Sawyer didn't want to be caught up in their way again as they migrated to better grass, so he stayed where he was until the dust settled, enjoying a drink from his canteen. When he came out of the trees he angled to the southeast, since the wild beasts had turned to the southwest. More than likely the natives would hunt them so they could kill some for meat and hides. He wanted to stay clear of the Indians as they hunted the buffalo.

The course he was on would take him to the Creek

Indian settlement of Tulasi, on the banks of the Arkansas River. He had stopped there on his way up to Kansas a week or so earlier. Perryman's Trading Post had a good stock of supplies if he needed to get anything when he passed through.

It took Sawyer another two days to finally arrive at Perryman's Trading Post. He tied his horses under a large oak tree, so they could rest in the shade. A crudely built water trough stood not far from a nearby well. He removed his hat and bandanna, then dropped the bucket that had a rope attached to it into the cool water. He pulled the bucket full of water out of the well, bent over and poured the entire contents on his head. The cool water was so brisk that he gasped, but it felt good in the hot July afternoon.

Sawyer poured three buckets of water into the trough and led his horse to it to drink. One thing he had come to learn about horses was that you always took care of your mount and treated him well. He was the best mode of transportation, unless you wanted to walk.

Sawyer entered the dark log-and-plank building that served as a store, trading post and grub house.

"Howdy stranger," said the man putting up some cans of food on the shelves as Sawyer walked up to the counter, still wiping water off his head and face.

"Afternoon, Mr. Perryman. I came through here a little over a week ago when I was headed to Kansas."

Mr. Perryman adjusted his wire-rim glasses and squinted at Sawyer. "I remember you now. You had a long beard and long hair and wore that old floppy hat."

"Yep, that was me. What have you got to eat today? And I probably need a few things."

"I've got some real tender beef meat and beans that you can have for four bits."

"That sounds fine to me. I'll drink whatever you have to wash it down with."

"Well now, I've got some shine and chalk or water."

"I'll have the water. It's hot out and it'll do me better. I'm not one for shine. That stuff is too strong for me."

While Sawyer ate his meal, Mr. Perryman asked, "What supplies are you wanting this time?"

"I'm not sure. I'm heading to Clarksville, Texas, and I have no idea about what's south of here, or how long I have to go before I can buy more provisions."

"You're on a long journey. When you leave here, you'll hit some rough, woody country and large, rolling hills and canyons. You'll have to cross multiple creeks and some pretty wide rivers on the way. They shouldn't be a problem this time of year, but if we get any amount of rain, they'll be something fierce for a few days."

"Where do you suggest I cross the Arkansas River?" asked Sawyer.

"I know some people that's been going across about a mile south of here, where it's shallow by the sandbars. The deepest part is only about three feet right now. You should be able to see where they've been fording it and if I was you, I'd follow their trail across the wet sand until you get to the other side."

"You said that I'd have other rivers to cross?"

"Yeah, there's the Deep Fork, the North and South Canadian, and then way farther south is the Kiamichi River. If you come across the Kiamichi as you're riding through the mountains in the southeastern part of the territory, you may want to follow it until you get back on flat land. There's a settlement in the far southeast part of the territory called Kuniotubbee. Three Choctaw Indian families settled it and a man I know has a trading store there."

"How long do you reckon it'll take me to get there?"

"I'm thinking about two weeks, give or take a few days."

"I only have enough provisions for another three days, so put me enough essentials in bags to get me there."

Sawyer's pack animal was so loaded down that he had to put some of the provisions on his horse. He left the trading post and found the spot on the Arkansas River that people had been using to cross. Although the river was wide there, the water was shallow and he made it across without incident.

# Chapter Twenty-Two

The next two days were spent maneuvering through the brush and scrub oak-covered hills that took him west of Okmulgee, which was the capital of the Creek Nation. The town and agricultural region had been devastated by the war. He rode west for a while before finding a shallow bend on the Deep Fork River, where he crossed without getting his supplies wet.

Several miles south after crossing the Deep Fork, he came upon the North Canadian River and made the decision to camp on the north side since it was getting dark. It would be a bad idea to take a chance and cross any waterway in darkness.

The sound of thunder woke him before daylight, and he went ahead and stowed his bedding on his horse and put on his slicker in case it rained. When he had his provisions loaded on the packhorse, he rode to the water's edge to wait until it was light. The rain came down as he sat on his horse and the longer it rained, the more thunder and lightning lit up the morning sky as the storm clouds drifted closer to his location.

All he could do was wait on the riverbank and try to keep dry until it was light enough to see. He left his pack animal tied to a limb and urged his horse into the river. It took him a considerable amount of time to find a path across the stream that wasn't too deep for the packhorse—he didn't want to ruin his food. When they reached the far bank, he turned around and went back after his other horse.

They climbed out of the water on the south side as the storm intensified and the wind picked up, blowing the rain sideways. A few minutes later he spotted a huge cedar tree and stopped behind it, out of the wind. The thick branches and dense foliage kept the blowing rain off him and his horses.

When the storm slacked off, he continued his journey, wanting to find the South Canadian River before the rain caused it to get too high to cross. With a sense of urgency, he made his horses go faster in order to cover the twenty or so miles quickly.

Late afternoon he rode up to the river and could still see sandbars, so he did the same thing as before—tied up the packhorse and picked his way across the cloudy red water. He tested three different locations until he found the best one, getting across and up the far bank without getting his food wet. After he had both horses safely across the river, he kept riding until he was clear of the river bottom. It was mostly one big marsh, and he didn't want to get stuck in there if the river got out of its banks and flooded the basin.

In the early evening, he made his camp for the night, setting up for comfort after a full day of riding. A nice fire glowed inside a circle of small rocks as he prepared his supper. Sawyer reflected on the past few days and thought about robbing the bank. He had been busy trying to get clear of Kansas and hadn't had time to count how much money he'd stolen from those crooks. He reached into the bag, pulled out the money, and separated it by denomination. The amount of cash he had piled on the ground when he was done was astonishing. He kept out two hundred dollars for spending money and put the remaining $36,800 back in his bag. It would come in handy for paying his part of the cattle-gathering expedition. The old farm had brought more than he thought it would.

He lay on his bed thinking about his sister and hoped that she and her husband would take the money he'd left for her and move away to someplace they felt safe. He knew that stealing the money would hurt the men for a while but if he figured right, they probably had backers from back east who supplied them the funds they needed to cheat people out of their land. Hopefully their backers would see them as a risk to their money and stop funding the operation. Deep down he knew he should have killed them and their hired guns, but he wanted to get away from that mentality of violence and become a law-abiding citizen.

The next four days were about the same. The terrain was mostly rolling hills covered in stubby forest with the occasional fresh-water creek. He kept seeing an abundance of wildlife—deer, turkey, squirrels, and sometimes the scat of a black bear.

On his sixth day after he left Perryman's Trading Post, the hills grew into small mountains and the ground got harder to ride over. It required him to think differently about how fast he traveled since his horse would have to walk over rocks and pebbles on the trail.

The terrain had changed to mountains which was mostly rocks, pine trees and some hardwoods. He could tell that he was now in the Kiamichi Mountains, where traveling would be difficult and slow. He'd seen plenty of mountains while on duty in Arkansas, and it looked like these were no different.

After a day of searching his way through the rough mountains, he figured out the best trails happened to be left by wild animals that roamed the area. Their trails took him along the valleys, where there was water and more vegetation for animals to feed on.

He followed deer trails most of the time and every so often would see one run away. The trails were narrow, but they provided him a way through the canyons and boulders. He had an abundance of water since there was a stream in each valley.

On Sawyer's ninth day of travel, he stopped for the night on the banks of a river and assumed that it was the Kiamichi. If that was the case, he should soon arrive at the settlement Mr. Perryman had told him about. He had to think for a few minutes before remembering it had an Indian name. Oh yeah, it was Kuniotubbee, the settlement by the spring.

His campsite was in a low, flat area surrounded by trees on three sides. There was a clear view of the fast-running stream full of smooth rocks, worn by years of water flowing over them. He hoped to be at the trading post soon since his provisions were almost gone. By his estimation, he had enough food for maybe three more days.

With his meal finished and his cookware clean, he threw a piece of green wood on his fire so he would still have hot coals in the morning. The night air in the river valley was warm and he didn't need the heat from the fire or a blanket, so he moved closer to the trees and gathered leaves and pine needles to lay his ground tarp on for a bed.

Too many nights on the battlefield had taught him to be cautious when going to sleep, and tonight was no different. He removed his two guns that he wore on his hip and placed them on the ground close to his bed. He took the .36 caliber and put it in his hand as he lay on his back and covered the pistol with a blanket. This was his nightly routine since he left Kansas. If someone did come into his camp, they would assume he was unarmed.

# Chapter Twenty-Three

The young traveler woke up but didn't move or open his eyes when he heard the faint sound that seemed out of place in the quiet night. He cocked the hammer on the Navy Colt in his right hand and waited to see if the sound came any closer. He could hear a faint rustle of leaves every so often and when he heard it again, he knew that it was probably someone sneaking up to his bed.

It was now a game of cat and mouse. He was the mouse, with a cocked gun in his hand, ready to play along.

Abruptly, something poked him in the stomach and a raspy voice said, "Don't move a muscle. I've got my gun trained on you, and I ain't afraid to kill you right here."

Sawyer opened his eyes and blinked to make sure his vision was telling him the truth. At first, he didn't know whether what he saw was man or some mythical animal. He was dressed in hides and buckskins and had a beard that came to the middle of his chest. The man had the longest, nastiest fingernails he had ever seen.

"Hold on, mister, don't shoot. I'm just a weary traveler on my way home from the war. I have nothing of value except a meager portion of food."

"I don't give a hoot about the war or whether you're a Johnny Reb or a Yeller Yankee. I want those guns, your horses, saddle, and all your supplies, is that understood? Or do I have to kill you to take them?" asked the man as he cocked the hammer on his rifle.

"I wish you would reconsider taking my guns and horses. I'll be out here without any way to protect myself and nothing to eat. How about I give you some food and you leave me be?"

The grizzled man pointed his rifle toward the two guns on the ground and opened his mouth to say something, when the blanket covering Sawyer's hand shook and a lead ball from the Navy Colt hit the man in the chest. He took a step back and tried to aim the rifle when the second shot hit him in his forehead, he stumbled backward a couple of steps and tumbled onto his back, dead.

Sawyer got up and checked to make sure he was really gone. The man stunk to high heaven from living like an animal. Sawyer grabbed a rope from his supplies, tied one end around the man's feet and the other around the packhorse's neck, and pulled him downwind from his camp.

He threw another stick on his fire so he had light to reload the pistol and get comfortable again. There had been many times when opposing forces had tried to sneak up on him during the war, but he'd never encountered anyone like this man before.

The next morning, he ate a light breakfast and loaded his provisions. It didn't take him long to get trail-ready since he was almost out of food, and he didn't have much to load on the packhorse.

The mountain man still lay where Sawyer had left him, although it looked like some wild animals had already used him for breakfast. Oh well. The animals had to eat also, and the man got what was coming to him by trying to rob an innocent pilgrim.

Some twelve miles farther south along the river, Sawyer rode up to a small trading post called Moyers and found out from the proprietor that he could ride due south and intersect with a road he could go east on until he arrived at Kuniotubbee. Sawyer bought venison jerky and hard biscuits from Moyers before he went on his way. It took him until the following day to make it to Kuniotubbee and find a spring to water his horse.

He made an early camp close to the spring that he had heard about. It was the main source of drinking water for close to fifteen or twenty families that lived nearby. He stayed to himself until after his supper and ambled over to where some men sat on the ground talking under a tree passing around a fruit jar of liquor.

"Hello, my name is McCade and I'm traveling to Clarksville, Texas. Could you tell me how to get there?"

One of the Indians pointed to the ground where they sat and said, "Sit down."

He picked up a stick and drew a crude map in the dirt. Sawyer studied the drawing.

"We are here," said the man, and pointed at the map he had drawn with the stick. Then he pointed his hand in a southern direction. "Ride the road that goes south to the next settlement about twenty miles south.

From there, continue on south past Goodland and cross the Red River. Go south of the river until you come to Paris. Turn east at Paris when you get there, and Clarksville will be a half day's ride from there."

Sawyer nodded his head and stood up. "Much obliged. Oh, and if anyone comes looking for me, I was never here." Sawyer handed the man a couple of dollars and walked off.

# Chapter Twenty-Four

Sawyer rode into Paris, Texas, the second day after leaving Kuniotubbee. He found a café, ate an early supper, and continued riding east until he came to the small town of Reno, Texas. There, he housed his horses in the livery and went to the hotel for a bath and a soft bed to sleep in for the night.

After breakfast, he picked up his horses and rode on toward Clarksville. There was no big hurry now that he was on a good road. Plus, it was extremely hot and humid in late summer and he didn't want to tire out his horse. He looked the countryside over, seeing a mixture of pasture and farmland. The soil seemed to be almost black here, compared to his part of Kansas, where it was a light brown sandy loam. Another difference he noticed was that the crops were mostly cotton and corn —no wheat.

Clarksville was alive with commerce as he rode down the main street that first afternoon of his arrival and stopped at the livery stable. "Howdy, stranger. Do you want me to feed your horses some oats and rub them down?" asked the livery hustler.

"Yes sir, I'd be much obliged if you would take care of them. And if you don't mind, can you stow my gear in the shade until I can do something with it?"

"I certainly can. You can put your things in that first stall. I use it for storage."

"Do you happen to know a few cowboys that returned from the war by the name of Ronnie, Hooter, and Cowboy?"

"Heck yes, I know them. About everyone in these parts knows them boys. I believe they're down there in the saloon," said the man, and pointed to the south.

"Thanks," said Sawyer, and handed the man money to pay for his services.

He walked across the street and down the board-walk a short distance, tipping his hat to a couple of ladies as he passed them. Sawyer stood inside the batwing doors for a moment before he spotted his friends at a table close to the piano. He started weaving his way between the empty tables toward them when Cowboy stood up.

"Well, I'll be doggone if it ain't Sawyer coming to join us." He left the table and gave Sawyer a handshake. Ronnie and Hooter did the same. "Pull up a chair and I'll buy you a drink."

"I'll have a big mug of chalk, but no liquor. I never acquired a taste for it," said Sawyer.

Cowboy hollered out, "Barkeep! We need another brew over here for our partner."

A woman who looked to be close to fifty brought the mug over and set it on the table. "When are you boys going to settle up your bar tab with me? I've got bills to pay just like everyone else."

"Now, Miss Lucy, you know we're good for it. We would owe you for the rest of our lives before we beat you out of one cent," said Ronnie before he gulped down a swig of his beer.

"Ma'am, I'll settle up the tab when we get ready to leave," said Sawyer as he picked up his mug for a drink.

"Who might you be? I ain't never seen you around here before," said Lucy.

"I'm Sawyer McCade," said Sawyer with a slight smile. He extended his hand to shake.

Miss Lucy took hold of his hand for a second and said, "Okay. I'll have the bill figured up so you can pay me what these boys owe." She walked back behind the bar counter and started gathering slips of paper from a box that she pulled out from under the counter.

"Thanks, Sawyer. We're kind of low on funds right now. We used our money to buy a chuckwagon for the gather. There's a couple more men who are interested in joining us, but nothing is final yet. We figured that they could put up money to help with supplies and such," said Ronnie.

"I see," said Sawyer and drank the remaining chalk in his glass. "Have you fellers put together a list of things we need to do before we can go after them longhorns?"

"Not really. We bought the chuckwagon because we got a good deal on it, along with four mules. We probably need to talk to the other men and put together a list of what we need. I know that we'll need a lot of extra horses so we can change out our mounts a couple of times a day," said Ronnie.

"We may have to start out with what horses we have since we ain't got no money left to buy extras," said Hooter.

"I can take two from my folks' place, but that's all," said Cowboy.

Sawyer pushed the empty glass toward the middle of the table. "We ain't getting nothing accomplished sitting here jawing about it. I say we pay up and go talk to those other two men, then we can decide how many extra horses we need to buy. We'll have to buy a lot of food, but I guess that's kind of premature since we don't know how many mouths we're going to feed yet. I sold my family farm back in Kansas and have enough money to fund our operation, so let's get started."

"Well, that's refreshing news! Sawyer has money and we can get started. I think we need another drink to celebrate our partner coming through for us," said Hooter as he raised his empty glass up like he wanted a refill.

Sawyer stood up and leaned forward with his hands on the table. He looked from one man to the next. "I didn't ride two weeks to sit in a saloon and drink liquor. It's time we get out of here and start making plans, or I'll go do something else."

Ronnie pushed his chair back and got up. "You're absolutely right. I'm ready to do my part."

Sawyer looked at the other two men still sitting at the table. "I'll pay that lady your bar bill and then I'm going after my horse. Me and Ronnie will be outside when you two decide if you want to be a part of this crew or sit here and drink."

He walked up to the main counter. The woman sat

behind it at a small table that she used as a desk. "Ma'am, how much is the bar bill these men owe you?"

The woman swung around on her stool and handed him a sheet of paper. "As you can see, they owe me nineteen dollars."

Sawyer pulled out his money and handed her a twenty. "Here you go, keep the change as interest and don't sell them anymore liquor on credit."

When Sawyer walked out of the saloon, all three men were waiting on him. "Sawyer, I didn't mean anything about wanting another drink. I guess I let the liquor get the best of me," said Hooter.

"Okay, but I'll warn you now, I came here to hunt down those longhorns and start me a ranch. You said that you've asked two more men to partner with us on the gather. I think that's a mistake. The more partners we have, the less we get out of the cattle we find."

"We're not sure if either of the two men will want to go with us," said Ronnie. "Joel Westman only lives about six miles south of town. We talked to him over a week ago and ain't heard one thing from him. I doubt that he can be gone from his place that long. His wife is pregnant and is due soon."

Cowboy spoke up next. "Sawyer, I hope it's not a problem, but the other man that's interested is a retired Union army officer by the name of Abe Jordan. He bought a nice spread about twenty miles south of here and has a wife and three kids. He's a really nice man and I think you'll like him."

"The war's over and it's time we put it behind us. I see no reason why I wouldn't like this man. You said he was an officer—what was his rank?" asked Sawyer.

"He was a captain and served under Grant," said Cowboy.

"Fine, let's go talk to these two. But anyone else who goes with us will be workers, not partners, and we'll pay them for their time. And that includes the cook," said Sawyer.

"I've been doing some checking around, and the going rate for a cowboy is twenty-five a month plus meals. I figure we need twelve men total to gather and drive the wild longhorns," said Ronnie.

"Okay, let's go see these fellers. Then we can start looking for cowhands, a cook, and buy extra horses," said Sawyer.

# Chapter Twenty-Five

The four cowboys rode away from Clarksville, making their way to the Westman spread. It took them less than an hour to travel the six or so miles before they arrived. The little house looked to be one large room and the structure was in need of repairs. Sawyer noticed the lack of upkeep to not only the house but also to the barn and fences around the yard and corral. His first impression of Joel Westman was that of someone too lazy to work. A lazy man would be wrong for them since they would have to work from daylight to dark in terrible conditions. He wanted to turn and ride away, but stayed to see what the man had to say.

A short, fat man with no shirt on came outside when the four riders stopped in front of the house. "Howdy boys, I reckon you're here to see if I want to join up with you."

"Yep, what's your answer? We need to get ready to go," said Ronnie.

"I sure would like to partner up with you, but I'll

have to pass this time. I can't be gone from home with the baby coming soon."

Sawyer turned his horse back toward the road when he heard Ronnie say, "We understand. You take care of your wife and baby."

The men caught up with Sawyer. "I didn't think he had the heart to be gone from home and work as hard as we're goin' to," Ronnie said.

"By looking at his farm, I'd say you hit the nail on the head with him. He's so lazy that he don't do any repairs around his place," said Sawyer. "We don't need anyone that's sluggish and can't pull their fair share of the work."

After riding another ten miles, Cowboy spoke. "When we cross this creek up ahead, we'll be on Abe's ranch. He's been working hard to fix his place up and make a go of it."

The difference in this ranch and the first one was as distinctive as daylight from dark. The house, painted white with blue trim, had flowers growing along the front and made Sawyer think this was a family that worked hard. The barn was painted red, and all the boards were in place—not a single one was deformed or cracked. A woman and two kids that looked to be about seven and four picked beans in the garden to the north of the barn. Then he noticed a baby bundled in a straw basket, resting in the shade of a peach tree. A tall man with broad shoulders and short gray hair came out of the barn. He had a leather apron tied around his front like he was working on something inside.

"Hello, Abe," said Cowboy. He pointed at Sawyer. "This is Sawyer McCade, the man I told you about that could be joining up with us when we talked a couple of weeks ago. We're ready to go after those longhorns, and we wanted to see if you were coming with us."

Abe walked up to Sawyer's horse and stuck out his hand. "I've heard a lot about you, Sawyer."

"Nice to meet you, Abe," said Sawyer.

They shook hands and then the four cowboys dismounted. "Come on in the barn while I put my tools up. There're benches so you can have a seat." The men followed him inside where he'd been working on a wagon. He removed his apron and put his tools on a workbench before he sat down on a work stool.

"I'm in, and can leave whenever you're ready to go. I have three horses that I can bring, but that's all I have."

Sawyer smiled a big grin. "I, for one, am glad to have you as a partner. I'll tell you right up front that I don't know anything about herding cows or being a cowboy, but I work hard and will give this my full attention. This gives us five partners. Ronnie thinks we need at least twelve men to make the gather and get the cows back to this area."

Abe nodded. "I don't have a lot of money, but I can put in a hundred dollars. That won't go far buying spare horses or provisions though. Do we have a cook for the chuckwagon?"

Ronnie spoke up. "I have someone in mind. His name is Blue Hickory. He has trail drive experience and I hear tell that he's a good cook. As for the chuckwagon, it's ready to go and we have four mules to pull it. If y'all are okay with it, I'll talk to Blue and see if he'll hire on. He should be able to put a provision list together for us so the store can start filling our order."

"I don't know anyone around here," said Sawyer. "If

a couple of you will take on the responsibility to hire us seven cowboys, then the rest of us can start buying spare horses. I have enough money to buy the horses and the provisions."

"I can help you with the horses," said Abe. "I know where we can buy most of them."

Sawyer stood up. "If you fellers will get busy on your assignments, then me and Abe will start buying horses."

# Chapter Twenty-Six

Ronnie, Hooter, and Cowboy left the Jordan Ranch to ride back to Clarksville.

Abe turned to Sawyer. "I'm glad to have you along," he said. "Those boys don't have the discipline that you and I have, and that could play a major role in how soon we make the gather."

"Yes sir, you're right about that. But from what I know about them, they'll work as long as we point them in the right direction and not let them get distracted with liquor. Can we go over to that tree where you have those chairs and talk for a few minutes in the shade? It's hot out here."

When the two ex-soldiers were seated, Sawyer spoke. "I assume you know that I fought for the Confederate army. Me and those boys fought together at the end of the war. I started out with William Quantrill and his raiders as a scout. In '64, when they had me trained, I was assigned to Brigadier General Thompson, Commander for the Army of the Northern Sub-District of Arkansas as sergeant and lead scout. I never rode with Quantrill or his men when they murdered innocent people. Although I did kill my share of men during the war, I wasn't a murderer," said Sawyer.

Abe looked at Sawyer for a moment, then said, "I'm proud of my service record and of the men I served with. From my own army experiences and from what I've been told about you, I know the kind of soldier you were and how you were trained as a fighter. But I'm here to tell you straight up that the war is over and I'm a citizen now, just like you. We did a lot of things that most men will never do, and we lived to talk about it. I honestly believe you and I have the beginning of a bond that'll make us good friends."

Sawyer removed his hat and pulled a handkerchief from his hip pocket to wipe the sweat off his head. "I'm trying hard to fit back into society, but it's hard when you've been taught to shoot first and ask questions later. That's something I'm going to need help with as we start our journey as ranchers. I'm good at tracking and planning out attacks, but I have a problem with trust and friendship. For the past three years, it was mostly just me and two or three other scouts that hung together. When it was time to act, we attacked and took no prisoners. That being said, now you know what I'm like and I would appreciate it if you would call me down when I get in that frame of mind. I want to get back to the man I was before the war."

"I have a word that I like to use in situations when I want to get someone's attention. When I call you Trooper, you're to stop for a second and think about what you're about to do," said Abe.

Sawyer put his hat on and walked toward his horse. "It's interesting that you've been in this situation before.

I suppose that I can learn to listen to you, but you may have to keep reminding me from time to time. Trooper... you know, I kind of like this idea of yours. It just may keep me out of trouble until I learn to take control of myself. Now that you and I are on the same page, I would sure appreciate your help in keeping me in line," said Sawyer and mounted up.

"How about we work together and see how it goes? Since you want to make some changes, you may be able to do it on your own. I'll go get my horse."

Abe led his horse from the barn and got astride the saddle. "Ride with me to the garden so I can tell my wife and kids bye," said Abe.

Sawyer followed Abe the short distance around the house and sat in the saddle while Abe dismounted and walked to the fence. His wife put the beans she had gathered in her apron into a bucket and went toward her husband. Sawyer couldn't hear their conversation but eventually, Abe turned to Sawyer and said, "Come over and meet my wife and family."

He dismounted and walked over to them, removing his hat. "Ma'am, I'm Sawyer McCade from Kansas. It's nice to meet you."

"Hi, Sawyer, it's nice to meet you too. I'm Kate," said the lady. She turned to her right and raised her voice when she spoke again. "Come here, children, and bring Ben with you."

The two children ran up to the fence. "I'm going after horses so we can start rounding up the cattle I told you about," Abe told them. "This is Sawyer McCade. He's a friend of ours who is going to be helping with the cows."

Sawyer hadn't been around kids in a long while and

didn't know how to greet them, so he just smiled and waited on Abe.

Abe pointed to the oldest child. "This is Card, he's seven. One day, he'll be a great hunter and tracker. Next we have Mattie, who is four. She always gets in the last word. And then there is little Ben, he's three months old and still sleeps a lot."

"It's great to meet you all. I hope we become better acquainted over the next few weeks," said Sawyer.

"Mr. Sawyer, why do you carry three guns?" asked Card.

That question took him by surprise. "My guns are cap and ball, and since I'm slow at reloading them, it's easier to have three of them so I don't have to reload as often when I hunt."

Abe changed the subject. "Bye, children, we'll be back later. We're riding over to see if Chester Mooney has some horses we can buy."

"Okay. Nice meeting you, Sawyer," said Kate.

Sawyer tipped his hat. "It's nice to meet you also."

They had ridden out of hearing range when Abe started to laugh. Sawyer looked at him, curious as to what was wrong with this man.

"When you answered Card, you pulled that out of the seat of your pants, didn't you?" he asked.

Sawyer laughed too. "I guess I did."

# Chapter Twenty-Seven

"Abe, you have a nice family back there. It's only me and my sister left in Kansas. My folks were murdered and their home burned to the ground, supposedly by raiders. But I think it was done by some men who wanted their land. The banker by the name of Hopson and a land company man by the name of McMillan have been stealing folks' land. These raiders come in and kill the owners and then the bank forecloses on the property. If I had stayed and investigated more, I would have put my sister in harm's way. Instead of doing that, I came here."

"I'm sorry to hear about your parents, but I'm glad you still have your sister. What's the law doing about the investigation and apprehension of the ones responsible?"

"As far as I know, nothing. I suspect they don't have any evidence, or they get paid off by the ones responsible." Sawyer wanted to say something about him taking the money from the bank and saying it was for the sale of their property, but he kept that to himself.

"How long has your family been living on your ranch?" asked Sawyer, wanting to change the subject off him and onto Abe.

"This is the first real home me and Kate have had. All the other places we've lived have been army installations around the country. An acquaintance told us about this ranch a few years back. We rode here and fell in love with it and got a bank loan. We have a few cows, but not enough for what I intend to make this place into. I want to take the longhorns and start breeding them to shorthorn bulls so I'll have a better grade of beef cattle."

"It seems like you have a vision for your ranch. I'm not sure where I'll settle down at myself," said Sawyer. "I hope and pray this cattle gather will help me decide what my future is."

"I understand. I'm glad that I had already left the army when the fighting that triggered this stupid war started," said Abe. "Brother against brother, that don't even make logical sense to me. But then no one asked for my opinion before they started a civil war."

Sawyer pointed to a herd of spotted cattle in a pasture they rode past. "What kind of cattle are those? I know they're not longhorns."

"Those are shorthorn cattle that belong to my neighbor, Mr. Byrd. He imported them from somewhere across the ocean. I've made a deal with him to buy a couple of his bulls to crossbreed with my longhorns. That's what he did a few years ago and it's paid off for him," said Abe, admiring the cattle as they passed by.

"So you think this feller we're on our way to see has

enough horses for the gather and the drive home?" asked Sawyer.

"I think so. I figure we probably need to buy twenty-five head if the price is right. Do you have enough money to pay, say, seventy dollars a head for that many horses?"

"That's a lot of money, but I can do it and still have enough for supplies and wages for our hands."

"You know we have to gather a lot of longhorns to cover the price of this expedition," said Abe, shaking his head.

"I know. But we can always sell the horses when we get back and recoup part of that cost," said Sawyer.

Abe pointed up the road. "There's Chester's horse ranch over there. Let's see what he has."

Abe and Sawyer turned up the lane that led to the house. A group of horses were grazing on the light green and brown grass to their right. Summer heat and drought had caused the grass to turn colors and stop its growth from lack of water. He noticed that a good number of the ponies were spotted, and that might mean that they came from wild mustangs.

As they approached the barn, they saw men in the corral with a horse that looked awfully wild. A cowboy tried to mount him. When the cowboy was in the saddle, the men turned the horse loose and ran out of the bucking bronco's way. He kicked and jumped, trying to throw off the rider, and even turned his head to try to bite the man on the leg.

Sawyer watched in amazement as the man managed to stay in the saddle on the bucking horse. The wild animal would have already put Sawyer on the ground if he'd been the one trying to ride it. The horse finally stopped bucking and stood still, with a wild look in its eyes. Its nostrils flared, taking in air, and the muscles in his legs and chest shook from working so hard. Or was it from fear?

A man waved at Abe, climbed off the rail fence, and waited until Abe and Sawyer tied up their mounts before he said anything. "Hello, Captain, who's your friend?"

Sawyer didn't give Abe time to answer back. He said, "I'm Sawyer McCade, from Kansas."

"Nice to make your acquaintance, Sawyer from Kansas," said Chester as he shook hands with both men.

"Chester, we need to buy horses that can work cattle," said Abe.

"How many do you want?" asked the horse rancher.

"We need twenty-five if you have that many," said Abe. "They need to be able to gather wild cattle in mesquite thickets."

Chester stood there rubbing his chin like he was deep in thought. "I most likely have that many, but it's going to cost you a lot of money. I'm thinking seventy-five dollars a head."

Sawyer removed his hat and wiped his forehead with the sleeve of his shirt. "We'd like to see these cow ponies and then we can talk money, if you don't mind."

"Mount up and I'll show you what I've got. I'll go get my horse and be right back," said Chester.

He returned with his horse and the three men rode a short distance to the south. When they arrived at a gate, Chester dismounted and opened it up so Abe and Sawyer could go through.

They rode toward a hill that overlooked a creek, and

Sawyer figured the horses were most likely nearby, since the grass was greener in the creek bottoms.

Sure enough, when they topped the hill, they could see a good-size herd of fifty or more horses scattered along the hill, grazing. A few of them looked up when the men rode around the animals.

Sawyer didn't know what to look for, so he found a nice shade tree and let Chester and Abe scout out the herd. They rode a circle around the animals far enough away so they didn't spook any of the horses. In a few minutes, the two of them joined him under the tree. Sawyer motioned toward the pasture. "What do you think about the horses, Abe?"

"There's enough to pick from, and by the looks of them I would be fine with most any of them, I reckon."

Sawyer removed his hat, set it on the saddle horn, and looked at Chester. "How much do you have in mind for each of them horses?"

Chester cleared his throat and reached for the canteen hanging off his saddle. He took a swallow and offered it to Abe, who shook his head no. "I'm thinking they ought to be worth seventy-five dollars each."

Sawyer pulled his bandanna from his back pocket and wiped his face just to start the negotiations. "I'm leaning more toward fifty-five dollars a head, since we want to buy twenty-five at one time. What do you think, Abe?"

"I'm going to sit here and watch you two haggle it out and be fine with whatever you decide."

Chester picked up the canteen again and offered it to Sawyer. "You may need a swallow or two to loosen up that pocketbook of yourn, young feller."

"Thanks, but I'm fine. You take another swallow and see if it helps you think in terms we can agree on."

Chester chuckled and shook his head. He hung the canteen back on his saddle and looked Sawyer in the eye. "How soon do you want to come after these horses?"

Sawyer looked at Abe for the answer, and Abe thought for a few moments. "I'd say we should be ready to get them sometime between two days to a week from now. Is that about what you think, Sawyer?"

Not being a cattleman, all he could do was nod his head to confirm what Abe said.

"I'll pick you out twenty-five of the best mounts I have and make sure they are all shod with good shoes for sixty-five dollars each."

Sawyer looked at Abe who gave him a nod. Sawyer rode up alongside Chester and stuck out his hand. "I'd say that's a fair deal. Do you want your money now or when we pick them up?"

"Bring me cash money the day you come after them."

"Thanks, Chester," said Abe. "We best be going. There's still a lot for us to do before we can leave."

"It's been a pleasure doing business with you fellers. By the way, young man, I do like to dicker, but you done struck a hard bargain."

Sawyer grinned and tipped his hat, then turned and rode alongside Abe back to his ranch.

# Chapter Twenty-Eight

Sawyer ate supper with the Jordans and when the meal was over, the kids, especially Card, asked Sawyer questions about where he lived and if he was in the army like their own pa. Abe finally told the boy to mind his manners and leave their guest alone. Sawyer didn't mind. In fact, it was the first time in three years that he had partaken in a family meal and it blessed his heart to have that closeness with a real family.

Abe kept pulling out his pocket watch to look at the time. "Those three should be back by now. You reckon they had trouble in town?"

"If I was a betting man, I'd say someone bought them a drink and they're in the saloon. And that could be a problem," said Sawyer. "I think I should go check on them and have a little talk before this escalates any further."

"I'll go with you. I'm not convinced they understand the importance of this gather. I'm not a drinking man and I'll not put up with it on the trail," said Abe.

Sawyer and Abe arrived in Clarksville after dark to

find the lawmen lighting the kerosene street lamps along Main Street. The two saloons were lit up and piano music drifted out from the batwing doors.

Sawyer and Abe tied up their horses on the opposite side of the street because there were no open spots at the hitch rail in front of the saloons. The saloons had a vacant building between them, and there wasn't much room on the street to tie up a horse if business happened to be good in either of the watering holes. "Judging by the number of horses out here, I'd say that business is booming at the saloons this evening," said Abe.

"It looks that way. It's going to be interesting what the fellers have to say for themselves if they're in there drunk," said Sawyer as they crossed the dusty street.

As the two men stepped up on the boardwalk in front of the first saloon, Sawyer reached down and slipped the safety off all three of his guns.

Abe reached out and grabbed hold of Sawyer by his arm. "Remember, those boys are our partners and even if we get upset at them, we don't want to do something that'll jeopardize the gather."

Sawyer grinned. "I won't kill anyone, if that's what you mean. But you can't count out the fact that I may get my dander up at them."

Abe patted him on the back. "Come on, let's see what they're doing."

Sawyer stood inside the doors while Abe sauntered on over to the table where Ronnie, Hooter, and Cowboy sat with two men whom Sawyer didn't know. He watched Abe point his finger at the men and say something. Then Cowboy stood up and said something back. Sawyer walked on over in time to hear Cowboy say,

"It's none of your business what I do. I don't take orders from no Yankee."

Sawyer walked up, put his hand on Cowboy's chest, and shoved him backward. "It's my business what you do, and you'll take orders from Abe, or I'll whip you like a red-headed stepchild, is that understood?"

A man at the next table stood up, red-faced and teetering on unsteady legs. "Cowboy's a friend of mine, and I don't like the way you're talking to him."

Sawyer pulled his right-hand Colt Dragoon from the holster and put the barrel of the gun to the man's forehead. He pulled the hammer back. "I don't know you, and I don't care who you are. You want to have a go with me, then let's swap lead."

Abe said, "Let it go, Trooper."

Sawyer never flinched or changed his facial expression, but remembered Abe's suggestion. "Tonight is your lucky night, mister," he said. "Now sit back down and keep your mouth shut."

Sawyer eased the hammer down and put the gun back in its holster. He turned back to Cowboy's table. Everyone looked shocked at the way he'd reacted. "If you want to be a part of this cattle gather, me and Abe will be across the street for five more minutes. If you're not there in five, then we'll find replacement hands in your place."

Sawyer walked toward the door with Abe right behind him. They were halfway across the street before Sawyer spoke. "I reckon that one word stopped a drunk from getting killed tonight."

"It looks that way. I don't know whether them boys will come on out or not. I guess if they don't, we hire what we need and proceed with our plan."

They had just reached the boardwalk on the far side of the street when the saloon doors opened and out walked Ronnie, Hooter, and Cowboy, along with three other men. While the six cowboys were still crossing the street to meet up with Sawyer and Abe, Sawyer stepped off the boardwalk into the street, raised his hand to stop the men. "Hold up and listen. I didn't come all this way to have my partners slack off in the saloon. I've just spent a fortune on horses, and we expected some news from the three of you on the cook and more cowhands. You let us down today. I believe in giving everyone a second chance and this is yours. There won't be a third. I vote that Abe is our leader, and he gives the orders. Now, do you have any updates?"

"Blue Hickory said he'd be our cook, and he's supposed to meet us in town at ten tomorrow at the store so he can give them a list of supplies," said Ronnie.

Hooter stepped forward and removed his hat. "Me and Cowboy hired five cowboys, and these are three of them. We won't be going back to the saloon until after the gather is over. You have my word on that."

"Okay, I believe you. Me and Abe bought enough horses to take with us," said Sawyer. "We can pick them up within a week." He turned to Abe, who stood to his right. "Abe, can you come to town tomorrow and meet us here to go over the list of provisions the cook has?"

"I'll be here. In fact, I'd like for us to meet at the livery stable where the wagon is at ten in the morning."

"Fellers, this is your last night to drink. I suggest you make the best of it because after tonight you'll be busy," said Sawyer. "Now get gone and we'll see you tomorrow at ten."

# Chapter Twenty-Nine

Sawyer rented a room at a not-so-fancy hotel for the next few days. He paid the clerk for a hot bath and shaved off three weeks of beard prior to settling in for the night. Even though the room he rented was plain, it had a comfortable bed, and it was after daylight the next morning when he threw the covers back and sat on the side of the bed and thought about how his sister was getting along. Maybe he should send her a letter or telegram, but he didn't know when he would be back to check for a reply. He shook off those thoughts and went to a small table in the corner of the room, poured water in the washbowl, and washed off his face with two handfuls of the cool water. The reflection in the mirror surprised him—his dark-brown hair had begun to grow out since the haircut in Kansas. His blue eyes sparkled as the morning sunrays came through the open window. He ran his tongue over his pearly white teeth and smiled at his good looks before he made a face by gritting his teeth together and sneering at himself in the mirror. He laughed at himself for having a moment of fun and walked away to put on his guns.

The morning breakfast rush was already over when he walked into the nearest café from the hotel. He ate his meal at a table by himself and didn't talk to anyone, just the way he liked it.

He wanted to look the chuckwagon over, so he paid the lady that waited on him and left. He thought Ronnie had told him they had the wagon stored at the livery. It was open, and the hustler and the owner of the place was mucking stalls when he went inside.

"What can I do for you, mister?" the owner asked.

"I thought Ronnie told me that the chuckwagon they bought was here. Do you have it stored somewhere?" asked Sawyer.

"It ain't here. It's down the street at the old livery that's out of business. I bought it some time ago and use it for storage. By the way, my name is Sid Sutton. What's yours?"

Sawyer stuck out his hand. "I'm Sawyer McCade and I'm partners with Abe Jordan and those cowboys I asked about the other day."

"If there is anything we can do to help you fellers, just tell me."

"Much obliged," said Sawyer. "It's nice to make your acquaintance." Sawyer walked down the street in the direction that Sid had pointed. It was a good distance to the closed-down stable. When he opened the two double doors, there sat the wagon. Sawyer slowly walked around it and looked at each little detail, satisfied with what he saw. He opened up the tailgate and it let down, like the cook would do to create a work-table. There were two water barrels on each side of the wagon bed. In the bed right inside the tailgate was a cupboard for small items, made for the trail so nothing would fall out or get damaged. The cover for the wagon lay on the floor of the bed, along with what looked like three or four tarpaulins.

He was pleased with the wagon, and although he had never been on a trail drive, it seemed to have everything they needed.

Behind the barn was the corral where four Missouri mules stood tall and strong under the shade of a tree. These animals were something he knew a little about. His family had used the same kind of mules on the farm back home—they were strong and stubborn but could go all day with little food or water.

Clarksville got busy during the early morning; he guessed the townsfolk wanted to get their shopping done before it got sweltering hot. Sawyer killed time by window shopping, and he even went into a few stores to look around. He stopped at the leather shop to see about a pair of chaps and new gloves, since he'd be driving cattle out of mesquite thickets.

A man with a boy of about fourteen were in the shop when Sawyer came inside.

The worker who Sawyer assumed was the shop owner stopped working on a saddlebag when he saw Sawyer and laid it on his workbench. "Howdy, what can I do for you?"

"I'm going on a cattle expedition to gather wild longhorns from the mesquite thickets, east and south of Tyler, Texas, and drive them back here. I need something to keep the thorns from sticking me in my legs."

"I have some nice thick chaps over here. You may want to try them on since they're all different lengths. I also have leather stirrup guards that work well to keep the thorns from poking through your boots."

"I'll look these chaps over, and I definitely want the stirrup guards. Is there anything else I might need?"

"I have a few Mexican lassos that are really nice, if you want to look at them."

"I'm not up on the term lasso. What exactly is that?" asked Sawyer.

"It's a rope made of braided rawhide and it's the favorite rope of Mexican Vaqueros. They been herding cattle for centuries."

"I don't know anything about cattle, so let me have one of those ropes also," said Sawyer.

Sawyer carried his new items with him to the livery stable and put them with his saddle. He found a bench under a tree and sat watching people scurry along, doing their business. The town environment seemed to suit him better than the farm life. Out on the farm, they would only get to go into town once a month for provisions. The rest of the time was spent plowing or harvesting crops. He had hated being a farmer and was glad to be a part of the new venture that he was about to embark upon with his partners.

He heard a wagon coming down the street—it was the Jordan family. Abe, Kate, and the baby were on the seat, with Card and Mattie in the bed, seated on quilts. Card and Mattie waved when they saw Sawyer. He got up and went out to meet them.

Sawyer and Abe walked toward the barn where the wagon was stored while Kate and the children went shopping.

Ronnie, Hooter, Cowboy and two more men came in from the south and all five of them turned toward the old livery barn where the chuckwagon was stored. The barn doors were open when Sawyer and Abe arrived to find someone inside, looking at the wagon. The man was bald-headed and clean-shaven, and wore a pair of overalls with a belt around his middle. On the belt were two knives and a gun.

Sawyer saw five men hitched their horses to the hitch rail and waved to them as they started toward the wagon where the man was bent over, looking underneath it. "What do you think of the chuckwagon?" asked Ronnie.

"It's a good one for sure. I'm Blue, by the way." He went around shaking hands with everyone.

When Sawyer had his turn to shake hands with Blue, he held on to the man's hand long enough to turn it over and look at his palm. "I'd say you've done a fair share of cooking and washing pots. Welcome to our party. I'm Sawyer McCade and this is Abe Jordan. Abe is the ramrod of this bunch, so he gives the orders. "

"That's fine by me. What store do you fellers use for provisions?" asked Blue.

"Use that first one you come to. I'm pretty sure they have everything we need," said Abe.

"I went to the leather shop today," said Sawyer. "I bought me a few things, like chaps and a leather braided rope. I suggest that everyone gets some chaps and gloves, and we need to buy some extra rope to take along."

"I have a list of items that we need to take with us, and I'll add those things," said Abe.

"Blue, did you bring a list of provisions to go on the wagon?" asked Ronnie.

"I have it right here, but I may need to adjust it. I

don't want to overload the wagon. I figure we can stop a few times along the route to restock."

"Ronnie, you go with Blue to the store and give them the list of supplies. Then you and Blue can start filling the water barrels and putting the cover on the wagon and get it ready to travel. Hooter, you and Cowboy find us the rest of your cowhands. Me and Sawyer will gather up ropes and the other items we'll need," said Abe.

"When do you want us to meet back up?" asked Cowboy.

"I don't want to rush it, so let's meet right here day after tomorrow at nine o'clock. That should give us time to have most of our things purchased," said Abe.

"I'm going with Blue and Ronnie to the store and leave the man some money. I'll meet you in a few minutes," Sawyer told Abe.

"Meet me at Swarts Gun Shop, it's two blocks north of the store," said Abe.

# Chapter Thirty

Canisters of gunpowder, boxes of lead balls, and patches sat on the counter where Abe had put them. The shop clerk was showing Abe several wooden boxes that he could use to keep powder dry when Sawyer walked into the shop.

Abe looked at Sawyer and then said. "Mr. Swart, this is Sawyer McCade, my partner."

"Hello Sawyer, I'm Richmond Swarts."

"Howdy, it's nice to meet you," said Sawyer as he shook hands with the man. He pointed to the counter. "Do you expect a war with them cows?"

"No, but I want us to be prepared if someone thinks they want our cows more than us," said Abe.

"Makes sense," said Sawyer. He moseyed around the store but didn't find anything he wanted. He still had a sufficient supply of ammo. "Abe, I almost forgot— I have a packhorse we can take with us. He can carry some of the things that we would normally put inside the wagon."

"That's a good idea. When we're ready to load the

supplies, we can put the tarps and tents on the horse to make room for more food in the wagon."

"Which one of these boxes do you think would be best to keep the powder dry in?" Abe asked Sawyer.

"I think the one on the right will work nicely." Sawyer pointed to the box.

Abe picked it up, sat it on the counter and started loading the supplies in it while Sawyer paid the shop-keeper. "Let's carry this ammo box to the chuckwagon, and then I best be finding Kate and the kids so we can get back home," said Abe.

Sawyer picked up the wooden box. "You go ahead and find your family. I'll take this to the wagon and check on the others."

"Thanks, Sawyer. I'll be back the day after tomorrow to put the final plans in place."

The two men went their separate ways. Sawyer stored the ammo box, then went to the store to find Blue and the store clerk filling boxes with salt, sugar, black pepper, cans of peaches and canned vegetables. Sawyer didn't bother them, so he walked around the store and gathered up another rain slicker and ground tarp for his bedroll. There was an assortment of boots against one wall and he looked them over, deciding to buy a new pair. He still wore the boots he found in Arkansas, and he still liked them, but the soles were beginning to show signs of developing holes.

He tried on four different pairs before he found boots that fit exactly right. He took them to the counter and when the clerk told him the price, he paid the man and asked, "Is there a shoe cobbler in town that can repair my old boots?"

"One block over is Arms Leather and Boots. He can fix you right up."

"Thanks," said Sawyer, and walked to the cobbler, leaving his old boots to be repaired. He wanted to walk around some more to break in his new ones so they wouldn't hurt his feet.

As he went by the saloon, he looked inside to see Hooter and Cowboy in a conversation with some men at a table. Neither Hooter nor Cowboy had a drink in their hands, which pleased him. Sawyer walked in and pulled out a chair to sit down at the table with them. Cowboy looked a little nervous about what Sawyer might do.

"Hello, men. Who are your friends?" ask Sawyer.

"These are the fellers that we're trying to talk into working for us," said Cowboy.

Sawyer raised his hand to get the bar girl's attention. "Bring us all a tall mug of chalk, miss."

"Y'all go ahead with your conversation, and I'll drink my beer and let you hire these men," said Sawyer.

By the time the mugs were empty, the three cowboys had agreed to hire on. This completed their assignment of hiring the seven wranglers it would take to make the drive. Sawyer paid for the beer and told the men he would see them the day after tomorrow at the old livery stable.

He retrieved his horse and took off heading south, taking with him one of the new lassos he had purchased. He hadn't said anything to the other men, but he had no idea how to throw a rope and catch a cow. He kept it a secret even from Abe, but now he was on his way to the Jordan Ranch to learn how to rope.

Abe and Card happened to be in the pasture on

horseback looking at cows as Sawyer rode up. He had spotted them from the road and stayed clear of the cows they were watching.

"Hi, Mr. Sawyer," called out the young boy.

"Hi, Card. It looks like you're having fun."

"Oh yes, sir. Pa is showing me what a pregnant cow looks like."

"That's good to know since you live on a ranch."

"What brings you back out here?" asked Abe. "Is everything okay in town?"

"Yes, it's all good. I found Cowboy and Hooter in the saloon, but they were sober. They hired the last of our cowhands. But I need help in the worst way. I have no idea how to throw a rope and catch a cow. I came out here to ask you to show me."

Abe smiled and gestured for Sawyer to follow him. "Let's ride to the barn and start your training out in the corral."

The rest of the day was spent teaching Sawyer how to hold a rope, coil it back up, and use his wrist to throw the loop. He chased a cow on foot inside the corral until he made a catch with each loop. He was confident and feeling good about his new skills...until they went into the pasture where the cows could run away. Time after time, he missed the animals and was frustrated until Abe stepped in to help. Abe gave him pointers on when to throw and how close he needed to be to make the grab. After a few hours, Sawyer was able to catch one in four loops, which wasn't bad for a rookie.

"That's enough for today," said Abe. "Let's go to the house and eat supper. I'm sure it'll be ready soon."

"You go on. I'm going back to Clarksville before it gets dark. I appreciate you taking the time to teach me."

"You should come back out tomorrow, and we can try heading and heeling. That's where one of us ropes the head and the other throws the loop on the back legs. That makes a cow fall to the ground and keeps them there."

"Sounds good to me. I'll see you tomorrow."

Sawyer thought about what he'd learned that day as he rode back to Clarksville. He was proud of his accomplishments and honestly believed he had a friend in Abe Jordan. The Jordan family had been exceptionally nice to him, and he appreciated Abe for spending his valuable time teaching him to rope. He tried to remember back to a time in his life when he had friends like that, who would take the time to help him do anything. The two friends that he'd joined the army with were that way; they'd helped each other with chores and work in the fields. But that was different. They'd done it so everyone finished sooner and they could play and have fun. He felt that Abe did it because a friend needed help.

# Chapter Thirty-One

Sawyer spent the next day with Abe roping cows, learning how to chase them down and forcing them to go in the direction he wanted. Both man and horse were tired to the core by midafternoon. Not only did Sawyer have to learn new things, but his horse had to acquire livestock working skills also.

Abe and Sawyer rode back to the Jordon house for water and rest since it was getting to be late afternoon. They had emptied their canteens earlier in the hot afternoon and both men were parched. Card met them in the yard and as the horses drank from the water trough, he ran to the well, drew a bucket of water, and set it on the stone ledge that surrounded the well. Card waved at the two men and took down the dipper off one of the posts that held the crossbar where the pully and well rope were attached and put it in the bucket.

"Let's go get a drink. Card has us some cool water over there," said Abe as he pointed toward the boy.

The men took turns drinking from the dipper and

when they were finished, Sawyer refilled his canteen and put the strap around his neck.

"By my calculations, we should be able to get the chuckwagon loaded tomorrow and the day after that, we can have Blue bring the wagon here. Everyone else can come on out and we can go after the horses and bring them back here until we leave the day after," said Abe.

"Will the horses stay close by, or will we have to try to pen them up somehow?" asked Sawyer.

"I figure by the time we drive them back here, they will have a leader and the rest will tag along. Horses will usually stay with the leader, although we will have a couple of riders that will keep watch over them so they don't try to wander off. I don't see them giving us problems once they figure out who's the boss and know that the riders will keep them bunched."

"Like I've told you before, I don't know much about horses and cows," said Sawyer.

"You'll learn fast," said Abe. "We'll have to have a couple of night riders keep them close to camp after dark. When we get a herd of cattle rounded up, then we'll have to take turns at night to keep them bunched together. Hopefully by the time we drive them back home, they'll be somewhat accustomed to us and trail without much trouble. It's going to be a hard, grueling job to round up those wild cows and get them back."

"Something I've been wondering about is where are we going to keep the cattle once we have them back in this area?" asked Sawyer.

"We can bring part of them here on my place until the others take their share and do whatever they intent to do with them. I can keep yours and mine here without any problems."

"That's good to know. I'm ready to get underway and learn how to be a cowboy. I kind of feel like I wasted the last three years fighting in a war that couldn't be won for either side. But the war did make me realize that there was more to life than farming dirt for the rest of my life. I may never make it as a rancher, but I'm going to give it my best effort," said Sawyer.

"I'm ready to get started also, so I can start my breeding program and have a better grade of cattle. Come on, let's go eat. Kate won't take no for an answer tonight."

"I don't want to make Kate mad at me, so I guess I better go with you."

After a delicious meal, Sawyer said his goodbyes and started to ride back to town. Tomorrow would be a busy day loading up.

On the way back to town, he thought of his sister again and wondered how she was doing. Only this time he decided to send her a telegram when he got to Clarksville. It would be a good idea for her to know that he would be gone hunting cattle for a few months, and she wouldn't be able to get ahold of him during that time.

The town's streetlights were being lit when he rode into Clarksville. Two deputies were putting oil in the lamps and lighting them as he rode past. The telegraph office still had its open sign in the window, so he went inside.

"Can I send a wire tonight?" he asked the operator.

"Sure. There's paper and pencils on the table over there." He pointed to his right.

Sawyer wrote out a message and paid the man. "If I receive a reply, would you make sure I get it? I'll be here in town tomorrow at the old livery stable and then at the Jordan Ranch the day after. I'll pay extra to be notified."

"I'll make sure any message you get will be delivered, especially since you're willing to pay."

# Chapter Thirty-Two

Blue already had a collar and breast strap on each mule by the time Sawyer got to the old livery the next morning. He watched as Blue put the bridle on the mules and hooked the saddle and breaching around their bellies. Last, he put the crupper around their tails. Then he was ready to attach them to the wagon tongue and string the reins along their backs to the brake.

Sawyer could tell that Blue had done this many times by the meticulous way he completed each task. The mules and wagon would be Blue's responsibility during the drive and the rest of the men would leave it to him. The same went for the cooking. They would all stay out of his way and let him do his job.

Sawyer walked up to the mules and ran his hand along the back of the nearest one. "Good morning, Blue. I see you're ready to get started."

"Yep. I need to know if these blasted mules are going to be worth a flip pulling the wagon. I'm getting them hooked up and will take them for a spin down the street."

"I tell you what, you take them for a ride and I'll meet you at the store. That way, we can load up the supplies when you're through joyriding."

"No one has said anything about getting medical supplies," said Blue. "But I reckon you ought to see if the sawbones will fix us up a kit in case we have any accidents. I'm handy at nursing minor cuts and things of that nature."

"That's a good idea. I'll see if Abe will do that when he arrives. I'm sure he knows the doctor here in town, if there is one."

Blue climbed into the seat, slapped the reins to the back of the mules, and hollered out a command. They took up the slack and advanced down the street with a jolt.

Sawyer walked across the street to the mercantile where their supplies had been stacked for them in the storage room of the building. There were burlap sacks of beans, rice, potatoes, and flour, as well as cans and smaller bags full of other things they would need. He stopped at the counter and said, "We're going to load up our supplies when the wagon gets here. If you will tell me how much we owe, I'll settle up."

"I have your bill ready." The store owner, a man by the name of Cecil, handed the store receipt to Sawyer, who looked it over before he pulled the money from his pocket and paid the man.

"If you fellers think of anything else you need, I'll be more than glad to get it for you," said Cecil.

"Much obliged. We'll let you know if we forgot anything."

Sawyer went out on the porch and sat down to watch for the rest of the men. The first one to show up was Abe, and Sawyer told him what Blue had said about medical supplies. Abe rode off to find the doctor. In a few minutes, Blue came down the street with the mules at a fast trot where they stirred up dust, followed by several riders. Blue parked the wagon so that it would be easy to load from the rear. He climbed down from the spring seat and let down the tailgate, waiting until the riders had tied up their mounts and walked to him.

"Hey, y'all come here," said Blue. "I need two of you to get in the back of the wagon. The rest of you start hauling out the burlap sacks first, and then the bigger boxes. Take your time and don't bring everything out at the same time, or you'll have to hold it while we get everything stowed and secured in place."

The men had started into the store when Sawyer remembered about his packhorse. "I'll be right back. I need to go get my other pony to put the tarps and tents on."

The men were still loading items when Sawyer returned with the spotted horse and pack saddle. He had a couple of the hands bring out the things he wanted to pack on the horse and stack them on the porch. When they had a pile of tarpaulin, ground tarps and some other cloth items, he said. "Hooter, would you help me put this on the packsaddle and tie it on? We should fix it so we can remove the saddle without having to unload the stuff."

By high noon, the provisions were loaded. Blue still had work to do putting spices and small things in bins and containers, but he could do that back at the livery under a shade tree. Sawyer led his packhorse to the livery, where he and Hooter removed the saddle so he could put the horse in the lot.

Abe came back with a satchel full of medical supplies. It was around one in the afternoon when Sawyer called out, "How about we find a stopping place and go to the café for dinner? I'm buying."

Sawyer led the way into the café and was greeted by a beautiful woman in her early twenties. "Good afternoon, gentlemen. I have a long table right over here that will seat you all. My name is Abigail and I'll be your waitress today. Can I get you coffee or water to drink?"

Sawyer made himself a mental note to come back that night and have supper in hopes that Abigail would be working.

After their meal, the six men walked back to the wagon and Abe told everyone wait before they went back to work because he had something to say.

"Tomorrow someone needs to help Sawyer put the packsaddle on his horse. A couple more can help Blue get hitched up and on the road. Then come to my ranch —from there, we'll go after the horses and bring them back to the pasture by my house. You will sleep at my place in the barn or where you can find a comfortable place to put your bedroll. The next morning we'll head out to find wild longhorns. Are there any questions?"

"Do you know the route we'll be taking when we leave your land?" asked Ronnie.

"No, but we'll discuss that tomorrow evening and everyone can have a say," said Abe.

Blue raised his hand. "I know a route that will get us to Tyler. I figure if we hunt east of there, toward Louisiana, we'll find more cattle than we can drive."

"That sounds good. We can talk about all of that tomorrow after we get the horses," said Abe. "I've done about all I can do here, so I'm going home. I'll see you in the morning."

Cowboy spoke up. "I assume you want us to bring the cowhands we hired with us when we come to your place?"

"I do. Make sure they have ropes, chaps, and gloves to wear and that they bring their bedrolls."

"Cowboy, you and Hooter go find those men you hired and make sure they're ready to go to work in the morning," said Sawyer. "Ronnie, you can go with them or stay and help me and Blue."

"I'll go with them and see you here shortly after daylight."

Sawyer helped Blue get the small items loaded into the wagon's cupboard the way he wanted. As he was watching Blue work, he saw him put a bag of peppers in one of the bins. "What do you intend to do with them peppers?" asked Sawyer.

"I like a little fire in my beans, if you know what I mean."

"That's fine by me. I acquired a taste for spicy food in the army. Just don't make it so hot the men can't eat it."

"Okay, I'll just use a little. We need to fill the water barrels, but I think we can do that at Abe's house before we leave," said Blue. "We most likely only need one of the two barrels until we get to Tyler. After that, we'll need them both topped off when we can."

"That sounds good to me. I'm ready to call it a day and have a bath—it may be the last one I have for a month or two," said Sawyer.

"Hmm, I figured you wanted to go back to that café. I saw you eyeing that pretty young thing," said Blue.

"I just might mosey back over there for supper after I take a bath. Maybe I'll get gussied up and talk to her," said Sawyer, smiling.

Blue sauntered toward the back of the old livery, chuckling. Sawyer walked to the hotel and took a long, hot bath before he dressed in some of the new clothes he had bought.

The café wasn't crowded when he sat down and waited to see if Abigail came to take his order. She came out of the kitchen door with a radiant smile and Sawyer was smitten by her glowing beauty.

"Hello, Sawyer. I assume you liked our food at dinner and want to try the supper meal?"

He gave her his best smile and said, "Actually, I came to see you, but now that you mention it, I will have supper."

"Well sir, I take that as a nice compliment, and it's good to see you also."

"How did you know my name?" he asked. "I don't remember telling you who I am."

"A little bird must have told me as it flew by. What are you drinking tonight?"

"Water please, and I'll have whatever you're serving for supper."

Sawyer finished his meal and looked out the window to the dark streets. Abigail came from the kitchen without her apron on. "Sawyer, would you be a gentleman and escort me home tonight? You know there are scary creatures outside."

This was his big chance to make the night special and see her outside the café. "It would be an honor to walk you home." He stood up, and they went out the door. She took his hand into hers while they walked along the boardwalk. At the next street they turned east toward a row of houses.

He felt like he was walking on a cloud and couldn't think straight. She stopped in front of a small house, turned to face the young cowboy before she said, "Are you going to stay around town for a while, or are you just passing through?"

"I don't rightly know. Me and those men that were with me today are leaving tomorrow to gather wild long-horns and bring them back here. I hope to start a ranch nearby. Maybe settle down and make it my home."

She moved in closer and kissed him on the lips. "That's so you remember this night. You come see me when you get back." She kissed him a second time and walked toward her house. He stood in awe of his beau-tiful angel, licking his lips at the lingering taste she had left. She paused at the door and blew him a kiss before she went inside.

# Chapter Thirty-Three

Sawyer tied the packhorse to the back of the chuckwagon so that he and the cowboys could go on to the Jordan Ranch. Blue would get there later since the wagon would go much slower. He could set up to cook for the men while they went after the horses.

"You men head on out. I have one small errand to run before I can leave. I'll catch up with you on the road," said Sawyer.

Blue looked at Sawyer and shook his finger at him. "You best go do that errand and tell her what you have on your mind."

Sawyer nodded at the old-timer and rode off toward the café. He walked through the door to find Abigail watching him.

"Follow me." She took him by the hand, and they went into the kitchen and out the back door. She put her arms around his neck and kissed his lips. He felt faint but loved every second of it and showed her how he felt by putting his arms around her and drawing her closer. After a couple more kisses, she let him go and said, "You be safe out there in the wild, gathering those cows. I want you to come see me in one piece."

"I'll be back and when I am, I want to court you and be your beau."

"Fine."

"That's it? Just fine?" he asked.

"All you need to do is finish your cow business. I'll be waiting on you, so get going and remember that I'm here for you."

Sawyer left town with a new sense of pride and purpose to his life. He had that feeling in the pit of his stomach like he would on Christmas morning, when he was about to get a present, and the excitement had been building for days.

It seemed like a short ride to the Jordan Ranch because his mind was occupied thinking about his new girlfriend. He caught up with the rest of the crew about three miles from their destination.

Abe's horse was saddled and tied up outside of the barn, and he was seated in a chair in the shade of the building, so they could go get the horses when the men arrived. Card ran out to meet the cowboys and Sawyer reached down and took hold of the boy's arm. He lifted him up so he could ride behind him to the barn where the boy's pa sat. Some of the cowboys watered their horses and filled their canteens before they all left to go after the horses.

Abe and Sawyer rode point with the rest of their crew spread out behind them with bandannas over their noses and mouths to keep from breathing the dust.

After they rode into the yard at Chester's ranch, a few of the cowboys watered all the horses while Abe and Sawyer talked to Chester.

"I have your horses in that pasture right over there. I'm goin' to be nice and loan you fellers my old stud horse to go with you. He's the leader of the pack per se; wherever he goes the rest will follow. I suggest someone use a lead rope on him and you won't have any problems with the herd. Don't let anyone try to ride him though. He don't take kindly to a saddle or rider."

"Thanks Chester. We'll take care of your horse and bring him back to you when we're finished. In fact, I'd like to sell the horses back to you when this is over. You should get a good price for them as cow ponies since they will be well trained," said Abe.

"Let me get my horse and a long lead rope. Sawyer, did you bring me my money?" asked Chester.

Sawyer reached into his saddlebag, removed a stack of money, and handed it to the horse trader. "You be sure and count it. I don't want to unknowingly cheat you," said Sawyer.

Chester held the money in his hand, feeling its weight. "It feels like it's all here. Give me a minute and we'll go after your horses."

Chester had everyone stop short of the horse herd and went on by himself. The big stud already had a halter on him, so Chester rode up, attached the lead rope, and walked the old horse to Abe. He handed over the rope.

"You men form a wide circle around the herd, and when me and Abe start toward the barn, you close in and the horses will follow us," he said.

Sure enough, when Abe took off with the stud, the rest of the ponies tagged along. Chester stopped at the barn and waved as the riders passed by. They traveled faster than Sawyer thought they'd be able to. He rode with the outriders. The dust wasn't too bad, but the men that brought up the drag looked like they were covered in dirt. He rode where they were and said, "You men hang back some more and maybe the dust won't be so bad. It looks like the horses are going to trail just fine."

The drag riders did what Sawyer suggested and backed off. Sawyer went back to his position and continued on until Abe brought the stud to a halt and motioned for Ronnie to take the lead rope while he went to the barn. The herd did what horses do—they started eating grass. Abe came back and put a hobble on the stud's front legs so he couldn't go off too far and then told everyone to follow him to the barn.

Once everyone had the saddles off their mounts and their horses were in the corral, the cowboys went to the well to pour water over their heads to wash off the trail dust. Kate and the kids brought them two buckets of chalk and clean glasses.

"Find yourselves a seat and let's talk," said Abe. "Blue, I see that you've got a fire going and pots hanging. I assume that you're feeding everyone tonight, is that right?"

"Yep, I've got food cooking and it'll be ready by suppertime."

"Good. You fellers can put your bedrolls in the barn or wherever you want to for the night. In the morning, we'll eat breakfast and then head south toward Sulphur Springs," said Abe. "The first few days, I don't plan on us making more than fifteen miles a day. Eventually we should get to where we can go twenty miles with daylight. I figure it'll take us five or six days to get to Tyler. We can restock while some of you go off in pairs and scout out where the cattle are. Are there any questions?"

Blue raised his hand. "Did you know there's a road that we can travel from Sulphur Springs to Tyler?"

"No, I didn't. If there is, then we can travel faster and get there even quicker," said Abe.

"Do you think a couple of us should go out about an hour ahead of the detachment and scout things out?" asked Ronnie.

"That's a good idea, Ronnie. Remember, we're not a detachment though—we're a crew going after wild long-horn cattle," said Sawyer. "That said, we should do it. You and I will go as scouts."

The men had been sitting on the ground drinking their beer and learning more about each other when one of the new cowboys by the name of Claude pointed to the north. "There's a rider coming this way."

Abe stood up and so did Sawyer, who removed the safety from his guns. The rider pulled up and said, "I've got an important message for a Sawyer McCade. Is that one of you fellers?"

"Yeah, I'm Sawyer." He walked to the man and reached up for the message. "Wait until I read this before you leave."

Sawyer unfolded the paper. It was a telegram from his sister. When he was done reading, he felt anger welling up. He had suppressed his rage enough to leave Kansas and he had hoped that robbing the bank would be enough to make the land grabbers stop what they were doing. He closed his eyes to try to diminish the rage within his heart, and the others must have noticed the look on his face because Abe walked to him and put his hand on Sawyer's shoulder.

He handed Abe the message, pulled money from his pocket, and told the rider, "You tell the operator to reply, 'I'm coming.'"

"That's it?" asked the rider.

"Yep, now go."

# Chapter Thirty-Four

Abe read the telegram and handed it back. "Why don't you go off and think this through before you make a decision about what you want to do."

Sawyer took the message back, nodded, and walked off to be alone. He stopped underneath a red oak tree, sat down and read the telegram for a second time.

*Not good here. They murdered Richard. I'm pregnant. We bought land. They want it. Need help. Come home.*

*Nancy Lou.*

He shook his head in anguish at how his sister must feel, pregnant and her husband murdered. She had no one to turn to. He knew that he had to go back, but he also had an obligation to Abe and the men.

The decision was harder than it should have to be, but it was the right one. He would let Abe hire someone to take his place and still foot the bill for the cattle expedition. He would have to forget about changing his life and instead revert back to his army training to survive.

Hopson and McMillan had money and hired guns

to protect them, and they used criminal tactics. Nancy said she had land and the men wanted it. Could he get back in time to help her?

He bowed his head. *Lord, I'm sorry that I haven't talked to you in a while. I need your help, advice, understanding, and instruction. My sister is in need. Help me make the right decision. Amen.*

He got up and walked back where the men were sitting on the ground.

"Abe, can I talk to you in private?"

"Of course, let's go over by the house."

"I left Kansas because I knew what I would do to those men who were running roughshod over the folks around Humboldt. I had all the fighting I ever wanted during the war. The banker and land man had their hired guns kill my folks, and the banker stole their land using a phony foreclosure contract. I gave my sister and her husband money when I left. Evidently, they bought some land that the banker and his associates want. They murdered my sister's husband so my sister would have to sell. If she don't give in to their scheme, they'll kill her too. I have to go back and help her. I hope you understand, but I can't let her down—she's all I have left. I've made up my mind that I'm going back to kill the men responsible for my folks' death and for Richard's. I'm on fire inside and they don't know what I'm capable of when I get this way."

"You take what you need and get going now. You can make Paris by tonight and be across the Red River early tomorrow morning. We can hire someone along the way to fill your spot. As for the investment you made, you'll have to wait until we return with the cows to get your money back, but I promise you that we'll pay you with interest."

"I'm not concerned about the money. In fact, I'm giving you eight hundred dollars to take with you so you can pay the hired hands and buy more supplies along the way. Abe, I may not live through this battle that I'm going into. The odds are stacked against me, but I have a set of unique skills these men are not aware of. If I survive, we'll settle up sometime down the road. You take these men and go gather those cows. I'm leaving the packhorse here and will only take a few items with me on the trail. I can buy provisions along the way since I know the route back."

Abe nodded. "Go ahead and gather up your things. I'll go tell Kate and the men."

Sawyer loaded up some supplies before saying his goodbyes. He went to each of the men and shook their hands, but when he got to Abe and Kate, he had tears in his eyes. "Thank you for being my friends. I wish I could stay, but I have to go finish this. I have a big favor to ask of you, Kate. There's a waitress at the café by the name of Abigail. Would you be so kind as to let her know what's happened and why I had to leave?"

"Yes," whispered Kate as she hugged him. "I'll be praying for you."

"Pray that God gives me the courage and ability to kill those men." With that said, he ruffled Card's hair and said bye to him and Mattie.

He mounted up, tipped his hat, and put the spurs to his horse, riding toward Paris.

# Chapter Thirty-Five

Sawyer wondered what kind of judgment might lie ahead for the men who killed his parents and his sister's husband. Those men and the men that worked for them put no value on human life other than to destroy and take what they had. He knew in his heart that this was going to be an almost impossible task to accomplish. Outnumbered and outgunned, he would have to get mean and fight them on their terms. He needed a plan, but that most likely wouldn't come to him until after he returned and had a talk with his sister.

Most of the businesses were still open when he rode into Paris since it was still daylight at eight at night. He had brought only his bedroll, coffee pot, and one small skillet with him for the long journey home, so he went into the mercantile and purchased the other provisions needed to accommodate him for a couple of nights. He could restock at Moyers Trading Post with enough food to get him from there to Perryman's store on the Arkansas River. That stretch of rough country across the Kiamichi mountains would be the slowest section of the trip, but at least he knew the area now. If he ran short of food, he could always kill a deer on the trail.

With his provisions tied to his saddle, he rode north out of Paris and headed toward the Red River. He wouldn't try to cross at night, but could camp close by and try in the morning, hopefully making it to Moyers by tomorrow night. He had a strategy—now all he needed was for the weather to cooperate until he arrived back in Kansas.

A few campfires were scattered along the banks of the Red River as he approached at dusky dark. He didn't want to talk to anyone since he was in such a foul mood, so he rode west a quarter of a mile and stayed north of the river to be alone. He built a fire so he could see enough to prepare his bed and warm up some biscuits and ham from the store in Paris.

He lay in his bed and listened to the sounds around him. Crickets chirped loudly nearby, while frogs made a ruckus from the riverbank. A gentle breeze blew through the trees and caused the leaves to rustle.

The cards had been dealt; he held them in his hand. Now it was up to him to devise a strategy that would deliver him the winning hand. He was never much at bluffing while playing cards—or in life. He only knew one way to play the game and that was straight up—just keep your opponent guessing what your next move would be.

The sound of his horse chomping on grass nearby woke him up. He eased the .36 caliber Colt off his stomach and sat up, tilting his head from side to side to work out the stiffness.

The sun had barely broken the eastern sky by the time he threw the saddle on his horse and got ready to ride. He would stop somewhere along the way and buy food for breakfast. First, he just wanted to get across the Red River and into Indian Territory.

He rode to the same location where he had crossed before. A family of six had a fire blazing, and the woman was cooking breakfast as he rode down the riverbank. She stood watching him, but never said a word or waved. He forded the river and loped his horse to the first settlement he came to.

Sawyer stopped at the town north of Goodland and ate breakfast there. He was surprised that it didn't have a name since it was a good-sized settlement with numerous businesses. Then he headed on toward Kuniotubbee, the town by the spring. He would bypass the main part of town this trip and go on to Moyers Trading Post. That was where he could get enough necessities to last him for the trip across the mountains.

The sun was setting in the west when he rode up to Moyers Trading Post. Mr. Moyers greeted Sawyer, remembering him from when he came through a couple of weeks earlier. "What can I do for you, young man?" he asked.

"I'd like to make camp and bed down for the night. In the morning, I'll need enough provisions to get me to Perryman's Trading Post on the Arkansas River. I'm traveling light this trip and figure I can make it in four or five days."

"Sounds like you're in a hurry," said Moyers. "I've got a barn and corral back behind the store. You can grain your horse and sleep on the hay. The wife has stew cooked, if you want to eat supper. I'll put you some supplies together in the morning and you can pay for everything at one time."

"That sounds good to me, thanks. I'll go ahead and take care of my horse and make my bed."

"When you're finished, come to the rear door. Our living quarters are back there."

Sawyer fed his tired horse hay and oats before he laid out his bedroll. He hid the satchel that had his money in it under the hay where he was going to sleep that night.

A woman who he assumed was Mrs. Moyers opened the door when he knocked. She invited him in to sit at the table, which she had already prepared for their evening meal.

"I appreciate the hot food tonight. It's been a long, hard day," said Sawyer.

Mr. Moyers came in and pulled out a chair. "I had three men stop by this morning heading north. You should probably shy away from them if you see them on the trail. I'm a fairly good judge of character, and I'd say those three are nothing but trouble. All of them wore Rebel uniforms and looked like they ain't had a bath in months."

Sawyer never stopped eating as Moyers told him about the three men. He nodded his head, but the Rebels didn't concern him at the moment. If he saw them on the trail he would go around them, but if they did try anything, he would deal with it.

When his belly was full, he pushed his plate to the side. "In the morning when you put me some grub together, I'm thinking coffee, jerky, bacon, and enough flour for just a little fry bread. I need to travel as light as possible."

"Instead of you taking flour for fry bread, how about I cook some extra biscuits and you can warm them up in your skillet when you cook bacon?" suggested Mrs. Moyers.

"I think that's a great idea. Can you make me enough for four days?"

"I certainly can. They'll be ready by the time you eat breakfast and get loaded up. You are eating breakfast with us, ain't you?" she asked.

"I'd like that very much. You're a really good cook, and a home-cooked breakfast sounds mighty fine." Sawyer stretched and yawned. "I'm going to the barn to turn in. Thanks again for supper."

# Chapter Thirty-Six

Sawyer stayed along the Kiamichi River until it made a bend toward the east. He took the same deer trail that he had ridden before. Mrs. Moyers had made him a sack of biscuits, and it was tied to one side of the saddle horn, and his other supplies were on the other. They would get in his way every so often, but he was glad to have the food for the trip. He kept his horse at a fast pace until the sun was overhead and then he stopped just long enough for a quick drink before continuing on. At the pace they were trekking, he would be to the South Canadian River by tomorrow.

He was able to make good time by traveling on familiar trails he had used on his way south. That night, he made a cold camp so he wouldn't give away where he was in case those three men Mr. Moyers had told him about were close by.

The next day, he forded the South Canadian at a low spot and picked up speed even more as the terrain changed from rocky mountains to rolling hills with scrub oak timber. He hoped to at least make it to the banks of the North Canadian by the end of day.

The horse had a good pace going when they rounded a bend in the trail and rode right through the middle of a camp. He touched his spurs to the sides of his horse and made him run, hearing the sound of gunfire behind him as he lit out.

He looked back and got a glimpse of three men reloading muzzle-loading rifles. If they didn't want riders going through their camp, they should've made it off the trail. He kept a quick pace to put distance between him and them.

It was almost dark when he rode up to the North Canadian River. His horse was tired and needed rest, but he needed to get to the other side before stopping. He went ahead and made his horse start across the red water. They waded in at the same location he'd used before, but this time, the river was a little deeper. He held his food sacks clear of the water and made it across in good shape.

By turning downstream and traveling a short distance, he could make camp at a spot where he'd have a good view across the river and the trail leading up to it —just in case he had unwanted company. This time he made his cook fire first, then stripped the saddle off his horse and staked him out to graze. He wanted to get his supper finished and the fire extinguished before it got dark. He was confident that the men wouldn't try to cross the river at night. That would be asking for disaster.

Sawyer was up before first light, eating the rest of the bacon he cooked the night before and a cold biscuit while in the saddle as he rode toward the Deep Fork

River. He figured he could cross it and bed down somewhere between it and the Arkansas River. At Perryman's Trading Post, he'd restock on food and feed his horse grain. The horse was tired and needed grain and rest.

The Deep Fork was low, and he crossed it with ease. The fast pace had taken its toll on his tired horse, so he made camp earlier that day to give his mount some extra time to graze and rest. He wasn't worried about the three ex-soldiers he had encountered on the trail. He had too big of a head start for them to ever catch up with him now. With his meal finished and his bedroll in place, he pulled off his boots, lay down and dozed off to sleep, only to be awakened by drops of water hitting him in the face a few hours later. This wasn't good.

He picked his boots up off the ground and shook out any creatures that might be sleeping in them and pulled them on. Moving as fast as he could, he rolled up the bedroll and found his slicker. The rain was still light as he scurried around to get his things in the dry. He placed his belongings next to a tree and set his saddle on top of them. With his slicker and hat on, he put his guns back into their holsters and sat down beside his things. The rain got harder, but he stayed hunkered down and fell off to sleep.

He wasn't sure how long he stayed in a deep slumber, but for some reason he woke up with a start. Something or someone had made a noise that woke him up. He hardly moved as he opened his eyes and let them adjust to the darkness. The rain was still falling, and it ran off the brim of his hat onto his slicker. With both hands inside the slicker suit, he gripped the handles of his pistols and pulled them free from the holsters. Whatever it was that had woken him up was still out there and if it happened to be the three men, he wanted to be ready for action. He eased the hammers back and positioned the guns so he could shoot with either hand.

A peculiar feeling came over him, like he was being watched by something or someone. He stayed still and took long, slow breaths to sound like he was asleep. In the dark of the night, he saw three figures coming toward him. They were more like shadows as they moved in his direction, but he stayed disciplined and didn't move.

They stopped, raised their rifles, then took a few more steps forward. They were still not as close as he wanted them to be before he struck, so he sat silent with his back to the tree and his head bent down like he was asleep.

He watched them spread out about three feet apart and come closer. They were within fifteen feet of him now, but there was a small sapling between him and one of the men. He waited until they came within ten feet, then suddenly he brought up both guns and fired at them. When he finally stopped shooting, he couldn't tell from the powder smoke and rain if they were all on the ground. He stood up, holstered both guns, and pulled the .36 caliber Navy Colt before walking forward.

All three men were on the ground. Two were dead and the other one had taken two lead balls to his abdomen. He was still alive, but probably not for long. "Who are you and why'd you try to sneak up on me?" asked Sawyer.

"We were going to rob you. Who are you, mister?"

"That doesn't matter none, now does it. You got what was coming to you for trying to steal."

The man gasped for breath once and died. Sawyer walked the way they had come, found their horses, and led them to his camp. He used the Rebels' ground tarps to build a lean-to so he could keep the water off and sat down and went back to sleep.

The next morning the rain had stopped, although the sky was still gray and the weather had cooled off noticeably. He packed up his things and covered them as best as he could in case it started raining again. There was nothing of value on the three men, so he removed the saddles and bridles off the horses and turned them loose, leaving everything behind.

By the time he arrived at the Arkansas River, it was rising fast so he rode on into the swift water and made his horse go across as fast as he could. Another hour, and it would have been too high to cross.

Perryman's Trading Post had hot coffee, ham, and biscuits when he rode up and went inside. He ate his fill and purchased the items he would need for another couple of days.

The ride across the Osage and Pawnee Indians' land was without any incidents and he made good time over the rolling prairies. Another herd of buffalo could be seen to the west, grazing on the vast prairie. He rode wide of the animals, stayed clear of any settlements, and made camp in a buffalo wallow that night where he was protected from the north wind. He could tell he was close to Kansas by how windy it was, and there wasn't much to block it as he tried to sleep.

# Chapter Thirty-Seven

Sawyer had no idea where his sister, Nancy Lou, lived anymore. He rode around town trying to stay out of sight until he pulled up behind the church. It would be good to talk to Reverend Toliver. He knocked on the back door. When it opened, he said, "Sorry to bother you, preacher, but I didn't have anywhere else to go."

"Come on in and we can talk."

"Thanks. I reckon you know about my sister's husband getting murdered?"

"Yeah, I performed the funeral ceremony for Nancy. She took it really hard, and so did the good citizens of the town. Did you know that she is with child?"

"Yes sir, she sent me a telegram. Do you know where she lives? I need to go see her."

"She and Richard bought a farm about two miles north of your old home place, and that's where she is for now. You should be aware that those men aim to have that place and a couple more farms one way or another. It's gotten worse since you left."

"What about the county sheriff? Is he not doing anything about the killings?"

"No, Sheriff Kiser must be on their payroll and so is the county judge."

"It looks like I'm at a disadvantage with getting any help from the law. I best be going so no one sees my horse out back. But before I go, do you know the name of the hired gun who's acting as the boss?" asked Sawyer.

"I'm not for sure and I don't like to gossip, but some of the church members think a man by the name of Lefty Branch is the foreman over the hired guns. He wears a two-gun rig, but don't be fooled by the name. He's right-handed, and that throws off anyone facing him in battle."

"Thanks, preacher. I must be on my way to see my sister. Please keep it quiet that I'm back, and I'll stop in to jaw with you when I can."

"Sawyer, let's pray for God's mercy and grace before you leave."

Sawyer removed his hat. "You go right ahead and pray. I need his blessing if I'm going to tackle those men."

When the preacher finished his prayer, Sawyer put his hat back on and left through the back door. Right before he got to his horse, Reverend Toliver called out, "I ain't always been a preacher. Sometimes a man has to be like David in the Bible. He has to stand up to the giant and slay him. You go do what the Lord leads you to do."

Sawyer nodded at the preacher and then tipped his hat. He rode toward his family farm mulling over the word that the preacher had said about David and the giant. He recalled the story from his younger days, and it gave him a sense of calm and confidence that just maybe God had wanted him to know that he, too, could slay the giant.

Workers were in the field at the old family farm, toiling in the heat, but he kept riding. There would be time to stop and talk to them another day. He had no desire to disrupt the fieldworkers, they were just poor people trying to make a living and feed their families. The men at the top of this scheme who gave the orders were the ones he wanted, along with the hired killers they paid to do their dirty work.

Based on the description he got from Preacher Toliver, there was a huge oak with the top split out from lightning. He knew he was at the right place when he saw the tree. Not wanting to be surprised by anyone other than his sister, he took care when he could see the house and barn up the lane about a quarter of a mile off the road. Sawyer reached down and removed the safety from his gun before he walked his horse down the grown-up lane that led to the house. Garments were pinned to the clothesline, and chickens scurried around the yard pecking at bugs. That was a good indication that no one was waiting outside to ambush him or his sister. It would probably be best that no one saw his horse in the yard, so he put the animal in a stall inside the barn but left the saddle in place in case he needed to leave.

He was almost to the house when the door burst open and his sister ran to him, crying. With his arms around her in a brotherly embrace, he let her shed her tears before he said, "Come on, let's get in the house. I don't want anyone seeing me here just yet."

"Thank you for coming back. I didn't know what else to do."

"Let's go in the house to the kitchen and make some coffee, and then you can tell me everything that has gone on since I left."

"I don't have any coffee. I'm almost out of food, and the store in town refuses to sell me anything. The banker and land man own the business, so they can control who they can sell to in town."

"Stay here in the kitchen. I have a few things on my horse we can use. I'll go get them."

Sawyer had gathered his meager provisions off his saddle and made it to the barn door when a man on a spotted horse came down the lane. Sawyer stayed hidden behind the open doorway and let the man get to the house.

"Mrs. Straight, I have a message for you from Mr. Hopson."

Nancy Lou came out the back door with a squirrel gun in her hands. "You get off my property, or they'll have to carry you off."

"Now, that ain't no way for a pretty little thing like yourself to talk to me. Mr. Hopson said to remind you that you have three days to vacate his property, or we'll bury you here alongside your husband."

Sawyer put his things on the ground, pulled his gun, and cocked the hammer back. He ran out of the barn heading toward the man and took him by surprise. By the time the man realized what was happening and went for his gun, it was too late— Sawyer fired until his gun was empty and the man lay dead on the ground.

"Oh my god," said Nancy with her hand covering

her heart. "You killed him! And now they'll come for me."

Sawyer went through the man's pockets and removed twenty-three dollars and some change. He stood up and reloaded his gun before he said anything. "They won't come after you because they think you're a weak woman who's not capable of killing. I'm going to load him on his horse. Then I'll take it down the road and turn it loose so it'll go back to town. That'll let them know that someone is out here ready to fight back for a change."

With Nancy's help, he got the man laid across the saddle and tied where he wouldn't fall off. Sawyer rode his horse and led the dead man's horse down the road past their home place. He slapped the horse across the rump with a rope and watched it run toward Humboldt. Sawyer rode back to his sister's and put his horse in the barn. That was one man that would never threaten his sister again.

He entered the back door to find Nancy at the table with her hands around a coffee cup, staring into the empty vessel. "Sis, are you all right? You look like you're miles away somewhere in thought."

"I'm fine. Sawyer, there're a lot of men who work for McMillan and Hopson in our town and you can't trust anyone," said Nancy. "I hope you know that there will be consequences to what you did today."

"I know. I brought the coffee in, so let's make a pot. Then we can talk," said Sawyer. "I have enough grounds for a pot or two. If you'll show me where you keep the pot, I'll make it."

# Chapter Thirty-Eight

Sawyer and Nancy sat at the table with their coffee. She was still distraught over watching him kill the man in the yard. Sawyer blew on the hot liquid and then took a sip.

"That was smart thinking spreading dirt on the blood spots in the yard while I took the horse down the road. The broom did a good job getting rid of his tracks, and no one will ever know that he was here. I don't think anyone will come calling, but you never know."

"Sawyer, I don't think you realize what you're up against with these men."

"Well, big sis, I reckon you need to fill me in on everything you know."

"We were asleep when someone beat on the front door and woke us up."

Sawyer held up his hand to stop his sister. "I want to know everything that has happened since I left. There might be clues that'll get overlooked if we don't start there."

Nancy took a sip of coffee and set the cup down.

"Two days after you went to Texas, I saw Pastor Toliver in town, and he gave me the money you left. When I got home, I showed it to Richard, and he was so excited. We had been trying to save money so he could buy this farm —it belonged to his aunt. Mr. Hopson, the banker, and Mr. McMillan, the man who owns the land company in town, had been making her offers, but she kept turning them down because she wanted Richard to have it.

"We came out here with twenty-five hundred dollars as a down payment. Richard agreed to pay the rest over the next ten years. She let us have the live-stock, along with farm implements for that price. We were so happy to finally have a farm that we could work, and he could leave the seed company. We met her in town the next day at the courthouse, where she signed the deed over to us. She stayed that night with us, and the next morning we took her to the stage line so she could take the stage to Kansas City where she has other family. We borrowed a wagon from a friend, Richard, along with two of his friends, moved our things out here, and we set up house. The next two days, he plowed in the field behind the barn—he wanted to plant milo there. The third day when he stopped for dinner, three men rode up to the house to inform Richard that Mr. McMillan wanted to buy the farm for twelve dollars an acre."

"Do you know who the three men were?" asked Sawyer.

"No, not really, but I've seen them around town."

"Okay, we'll get back to them later. Go on."

"Richard was a good man, but he wasn't a violent person and when they told him the offer, he said he wasn't interested in that price. We had paid more than that for the land. The men turned their horses around and rode off without saying another word. I told Richard that we needed to keep a gun handy because they could be the same men who killed my folks and burned their home."

"Back to these men. Can you describe them to me? Or describe the horses they were riding?"

"I don't remember much about that day. I never came outside, but I did look out the window. The man doing the talking rode a buckskin horse and was dressed in nice black clothes. I don't know what the other two looked like or what they rode."

Sawyer took a drink of his coffee and took hold of his sister's hand. "I know this is hard on you, but I need to know every detail you can think of."

She took a sip from her own cup and wiped her eyes with a handkerchief. "The next day, we took the wagon into town for seed and groceries and to drop off a couple of tools that needed repairing at the blacksmith shop. We bought the seed from Richard's former employer and then went to the mercantile for groceries. While Richard loaded the supplies in the wagon, two men came up and started giving him a hard time about not selling the farm to Mr. McMillan. When he tried to walk back into the store, one of the men hit him in the face. It knocked him to the ground. I ran to him, and one man told the other one to cut open the seed sacks. They were laughing the whole time they destroyed our seed."

"Do you know who the two men were, or have you seen them since?"

"No, I had never seen them before that day, but I have seen them since. The man who hit Richard was missing his left thumb. I thought it was rather odd that a man would be missing a thumb since he wore two guns."

Sawyer pounded the table with his fist. "That's something I can use to recognize them when I'm in town! Go on with your story."

"We went back to the seed store so Richard could buy more seed. We didn't have any more incidents that day. The next two days he worked in the field plowing and planting the milo. The evening of the third day, the same three men rode back out and told Richard they brought the final offer to buy the land. Mr. McMillan's final offer was fourteen dollars an acre. Richard politely turned them down and I strongly remember what the man said. He said, 'You're making a big mistake. Mr. McMillan has made you a fair offer and now you will suffer the consequences.'"

"What did they do after that?" asked Sawyer.

"They left. I begged Richard to sell it to McMillan; we could relocate somewhere else. I was afraid the same thing that happened to Mama and Papa would happen here. Richard wouldn't hear of it, and it made him mad when I told him my fears. He did agree to put his squirrel gun close to the door in case they came back. He finished planting the next day, and that night he commented that they were just trying to intimidate him into selling. Once the crops came up and were harvested, he would sell them, and McMillan would leave us alone."

The two of them sat in silence and finished their coffee.

"Sawyer," said Nancy. "My husband was naïve. He always tried to see the good in people, and that's what got him killed. We were awakened sometime after midnight by someone pounding on the front door."

"You said the front door, is that right?" asked Sawyer.

"Yes, the front door. We heard the person call out for help. Richard went to the door and opened it, but no one was there. I told him to close it and step away from it, but he stepped out onto the porch, and that was when I heard a blast and saw a huge flash of light. They shot him with a double-barrel shotgun. I don't remember much after that."

Sawyer let her wipe the tears from her eyes and compose herself before he asked, "Did you see anyone or hear them leave?"

"No, I was so distraught that I don't remember anything."

"What happened after that?"

"I finally rode into town, went to Sheriff Kiser's office, and reported it. He sent the undertaker out to collect the body. The next day we had a funeral and buried him in the town cemetery."

"What did the sheriff say or do about it?"

"Nothing. He never came out here to investigate nor asked any questions that I know of. All he said to me was that it was probably someone passing by that did it. After the funeral, I went to the mercantile to buy supplies, and Mr. Adams told me that he couldn't sell me anything. When I asked him why, he just walked off. Three days ago, the same three men came by and made me another offer of fifteen dollars an acre. I told them that I would think about it. Now you're caught up on everything, right up to when you shot that man."

"Speaking of him, has he been out here before, or had you ever seen him in town before?"

"Not that I can remember."

"I'm riding back into town tonight to have a look around and talk to Reverend Toliver. I trust him, and he'll keep quiet that I'm here. I'll also have a talk with Mr. Adams at the mercantile and see why he can't sell you provisions. Make me a list of things you need, and I'll buy them while I'm there."

"I wish you wouldn't go into town and leave me here alone. They may see you and try to kill you, like they do everyone who crosses them. It's rumored that they've taken at least eight farms since they've been in business here."

"I'll be fine in town, and you'll be okay until I get back. I'm well aware of who I'm dealing with, but they have no idea of the skills that I possess. I'm not one to take prisoners in battle. You will see that I'm an aggressor who shows no mercy. When they find the man I killed today, it will make them a little uneasy not knowing exactly who killed him and why, so that gives us a day or two to do some things."

"Did you know that the bank got robbed about the time you left town a few weeks ago?" asked Nancy.

Sawyer scooted back in his chair and then looked her in the eyes. "Yes, I knew it got robbed before I left town."

Nancy sighed and closed her eyes tightly. Then she opened them and said, "I have to know, Sawyer. Is that where the money came from that you left us?"

He looked at her but said nothing, then got up from the chair. "Don't shoot me when I come back later. It'll probably be after dark. I think I'll stay in the barn tonight so I can watch the house from there."

"You're all I have left, and I don't want you getting hurt, so you make sure to watch your back with these men."

Sawyer gave his sister a kiss on the cheek and went out the door.

# Chapter Thirty-Nine

Sawyer rode to his folks' farm. When he arrived, there were people working in the field, so he rode out to talk to them. He could tell they were nervous by the way they kept stealing quick glances toward the burned-out house. Perhaps there was someone there watching them work.

"Sorry to bother you, but could you tell me who you work for?" asked Sawyer.

"We ain't supposed to talk to anyone while we work," said the husband and father of the ones hoeing the field. He looked toward the charred ruins again, like he didn't want to be seen talking.

"Is there someone at the old home place watching you work? I notice you keep looking that way," asked Sawyer.

"Mister, you could get us fired if he sees you out here."

"Tell me what I want to know, and I'll leave. Who do you work for, and what's the name of the person who's supposed to be watching you?"

"Mr. Hopson owns the farm and his foreman is Lucas Killian. Now please go before Lucas gets back."

"Much obliged," said Sawyer, and rode back to the road and continued toward town. He had traveled close to a mile when he saw a man on a horse coming his way. He removed the safety from his gun and pulled it from the holster in case there was trouble.

"Howdy, friend. Can you tell me how far it is to Humboldt?" asked Sawyer when he was within talking distance of the rider.

"Who are you, and what's your business there?" asked the man in a hateful tone.

Sawyer pointed his gun at the man's chest. "Mister, I don't think it's any of your business who I am and what my affairs are in town. And I really don't think you want to make it your concern."

The man threw up his hands. "Now hold on! I didn't mean to get your dander up. Town is about another mile or so down the road."

"What's your name?" asked Sawyer.

"Lucas Killian. I oversee a couple of farms around here."

Sawyer holstered his gun, deciding not to give away too much about what he was up to. "I don't have any business in town, I'm just passing through." He touched the spurs to his horse and rode on past Lucas.

The first stop in town was the church. He knocked on the back door and waited, but when no one opened it, he went to the parsonage. Mrs. Toliver came to the door.

"Good afternoon, ma'am. Is the preacher in?" asked Sawyer.

"No, he's gone out to the Sampson place. Loretta is sick, and they requested prayer."

"Thank you. In that case, I reckon I'll talk to him later."

Sawyer knew where the Sampson place was, so he rode that way hoping he would meet the preacher on the road somewhere. The Sampsons lived east of town about two miles. He was almost to the house when he saw a buckboard coming his way, so he stopped to see if it was Reverend Toliver. As soon as he recognized the man, Sawyer gave him a wave.

"Hello, Sawyer, what brings you out here?" asked the reverend as he rode up and stopped next to Sawyer's horse.

"I came to ask you a few questions, if that's all right," said Sawyer.

"It is, but we need to get off the road. One of their hired guns came into town today tied to his saddle full of lead. They're in an uproar about who could have killed him, and men are watching everything around town. There's a spot not far ahead that we can use." They took off toward a lane that led to an abandoned house.

"I've been talking to my sister," said Sawyer. "She told me that three men have come to her house three different times with offers to purchase her land. The man that does the talking rides a buckskin horse. Do you happen to know who he is?"

"Yep," said the preacher. "I know that one. That's Bucky, and he's one of McMillan's top men. He likes to run roughshod over the townsfolk. Most of them are afraid of him and his two men. I believe one of them is named Kelly and the other one is Fargo. That Fargo feller is supposed to be fast with a gun, and rumor is, he's killed six men in gunfights."

"Do you know anything about Lucas Killian?" asked Sawyer.

"Lucas is the foreman over most of the stolen farmland. He's a coarse man to deal with and has a reputation of hitting his workers and intimidating them into silence. He's a rouser that came in here from back east with Nathaniel Hopson."

"Nancy told me that she went to the county sheriff when Richard was murdered. He didn't come to her house and investigate; all he did was send the undertaker for the body. What do you know about Sheriff Kiser?"

"He's as crooked as they come and a disgrace to the badge he wears. Hopson and McMillan tell him what to do and when to do it. They got him elected a couple of years ago and now everyone is scared to run against him." The preacher slapped his hand against the seat. "I just had an idea! Why don't you run for county sheriff? The election is in two weeks and the filing period is open until five o'clock tomorrow. You run for sheriff, and I guarantee that the hoodlums and killers will show themselves. They'll stop at nothing to make sure you don't get elected."

"Hmm." Sawyer took a drink of water from his canteen. "That's an interesting idea. I'll think about it," he said. "That could be a game-changer if I happened to win and start my own lawful investigation. I'm sure that Hopson and McMillan have support from back east with lots of money. Have you ever heard who that might be?"

"No, that's information I know nothing about. All I

know is when the bank was robbed, they had more money in a few days to stay in business."

"What do you know about the telegraph operator? Is he one of their men?"

"Bolton has been here as long as I can remember. I'm sure they've threatened him about keeping people's privacy, but he's always been good about the confidentiality of messages that come and go."

"Who's the county judge?" asked Sawyer.

"That would be Judge Homer Elliott. He signs all the repossession papers and grants new deeds to the land they steal. I don't have any use for that man."

Sawyer scratched his chin in thought. "That's pretty much all the questions I have for you today, but would it be all right if I come to you in the future for information? You're the only person I trust in town."

"You can ask me anything and I'll try to help. Just be careful around town. They have people on the payroll everywhere."

"Thanks again. I best be going. I need to pick up some supplies for Nancy."

"One more thing," said the preacher. "Rumor around town is that they also bought out Adam's Mercantile but kept him on to operate it as manager."

"Yeah, I figured as much from what Nancy told me. I was going there to buy my things, but I might have to find another place to shop."

"I'm afraid they'll buy up all the necessary businesses and choke this town out of everything people have worked their whole lives for," said the preacher.

"You may be right. Well, I'll be seeing you," said Sawyer. "You head on out, and I'll give you a few minutes before I ride back to town myself."

# Chapter Forty

Sawyer tied his horse in front of Adams Mercantile and went inside. A couple of women were shopping the aisles and looking at bolts of fabric. Sawyer walked up to the counter and put his list on the worn wooden countertop. "Are you Mr. Adams?"

"Yes, I am," he said, looking at Sawyer's list. "Would you like this filled?"

"Yes. And if you don't mind, add a canister of gunpowder, wads, and two boxes of .44 and .36 caliber lead balls," said Sawyer.

"Yes sir, coming right up."

Sawyer looked around the store and when the clerk had his items on the counter, he motioned to Sawyer.

"Put everything in a couple of burlap sacks. I'm on a horse," said Sawyer.

"I'll be right back with your sacks." The stork clerk went into the back room, and the two women walked by Sawyer going toward the door. He tipped his hat at them and smiled, then turned back around to watch for Mr. Adams. The clerk came in and put everything in two sacks like Sawyer had asked for. "That'll be $7.22," he said.

Sawyer counted out the money and put it on the counter but kept his left hand on it. "You don't remember me, do you, Alexander?" The man's head shot up, and he looked at Sawyer with fright in his eyes.

"No, I don't remember you. Should I?"

"Can you keep a secret?"

Alexander Adams nodded his head. He looked into Sawyer's unfriendly eyes and then down at the money, still under his hand.

"I'm Nancy Lou's brother, Sawyer. I've come back to town to get revenge on the men who murdered our folks and her husband. I've only been here one day and I'm already hearing rumors that you sold out to Hopson and is now working for him. As I said earlier, I'm here for revenge. If I find out you lied to me, I'll come for you also. Did you sell to Hopson?"

Alexander was white as a bleached sheet and rubbed his hand over his mouth. "You can't tell a soul about this, swear to me."

Sawyer nodded his head to confirm yes. "Get to talking."

"I was forced to sell out to Hopson. I had a bank loan, and they were going to foreclose on my store and house if I didn't sell. Judge Elliott had already signed the papers allowing them to do it. Sawyer, I didn't have a choice in the matter."

"Who comes around and checks on how you're doing or gives you instructions?"

"That would be Lesley Overstreet. He goes by Les and he's a gunfighter they brought in from Missouri. He rode with Quantrill and his raiders during the war. It's rumored that he was in on the massacre in Lawrence."

"Do you know of any more businesses that they've stolen?" asked Sawyer.

"I'm almost certain they have the telegraph office and maybe the newspaper."

"Thanks, you've been a big help. If anyone asks, you don't know me. But I'll let you in on a little secret. I'm running for county sheriff in two weeks."

"If you run, they'll come after you and try to kill you. You won't be able to buy any campaign ads or signs anywhere in town."

"I know. That's why I'm telling you—so you can start spreading the word to the good folks in town. But wait until after tomorrow. Remember, don't let their hired men know that you know me."

"My lips are sealed."

Sawyer tied his sacks on his saddle and rode east out of town. He waited until he was out of sight from anyone that could have been watching, turned south, and rode back to his sister's farm.

# Chapter Forty-One

Sawyer placed the two burlap sacks of provisions on the kitchen table. "I'll take my horse to the barn while you get supper started. After supper, we can talk about what I found out in Humboldt."

"Okay, I'll get to cooking. If you don't mind, will you feed the chickens and close the door to the chicken coop?"

"Of course I will. I'll go ahead and arrange a place to sleep in the barn. I need to be able to move freely around the barn and yard in case someone comes to the house."

"Do you think they'll return tonight?" she asked, frowning.

"I'm not taking any chances with that bunch. We'll talk more about it after supper, but right now I need to get things prepared for tonight."

Sawyer unsaddled his horse, fed him some hay, and left him inside the barn in one of the stalls. He took his own rope and another one he found in the barn and tied them together. Then he took them down the lane away from the house a hundred feet and tied them as tight as he could between two trees so that the rope ran across the width of the narrow road.

In the burn barrel, he found two empty cans and put a couple of rocks in each one before tying them to the ropes with twine. Back inside the barn, he put hay against the front inside wall close to the door and lay his ground tarp on it, and then his bedroll. He would be ready if trouble came their way during the night.

Nancy filled him a plate of fried potatoes and ham when he came inside and sat down at the table. "Thanks for cooking this late. I had so much to do that time got away from me in town."

"Eat up, and let's talk. I'm curious to hear what you found out today."

When they had finished eating and were on their second cups of coffee, Sawyer told her what he had found out and the names of the men who had come to her farm. He also told her about his conversation with Mr. Adams.

"I knew something was up. He was always so accommodating, and then all of a sudden he didn't want my business."

"Did you know that the election for sheriff is in two weeks?"

"No, but what does that have to do with anything?" she asked, confused.

"You know that Sheriff Kiser and Judge Elliott are crooked and they're on Hopson's payroll. So, I'm going back to town tomorrow afternoon to file as a candidate for county sheriff."

"No, you can't do that! They'll come after you and

kill you. You said they want to take over the town and they will not let you get elected."

"Sis, I've thought this out, and the only way I can pull this off is to come at them in a way that they don't expect. I'm aware that they'll send their hired guns after me, but they underestimate my capabilities. I'll be the aggressor and hit them when they least expect it."

"Sawyer, you're all I have left, and I want my baby to know its uncle. What will we do if they come here when you're gone to town or out doing other things?"

"I've been thinking about that. I want to take you to Iola and put you in a boarding house there. No one will know who you are and we'll give them a fake name. You can tell them that you're there until the carpenters have your new house completed. Hopson's men won't search for you there, and I can have plenty of room to inflict my form of judgment."

"But what if they come and burn down the house while I'm gone?"

"I'm going to stay in the barn out of sight. If they come back and see that you're gone, I think they'll figure you packed up and left out of fear. If they try to set the house on fire, I'll kill whoever tries."

She rubbed her hands on her face. "Okay, I'll do what you want. I trust your judgment. When do you want to take me to Iola?"

"I'll harness up your wagon first thing in the morning and take you there before I ride into Humboldt."

"I would rather you saddle the horse in the pasture and let me ride it. That wagon is so rough that it makes my bottom sore."

"That's fine, I'll have it ready in the morning. I tied

a rope across the road with cans tied to it, so they'll rattle if we have company tonight."

"I saw you walk down the lane and wondered what you were doing."

"I thought I'd give them a little surprise if they want to come calling. I'm tired, so I'm going to the barn and going to sleep. If you hear anything at all tonight, get on the floor until you hear from me. Otherwise, I'll see you in the morning after I care for your animals."

# Chapter Forty-Two

Sawyer left Nancy Lou at the boarding house in Iola and rode back to Humboldt to talk to the telegraph operator. He felt like the man could still keep a secret since no one in town knew that he'd come back and help his sister. If the operator had told Hopson or McMillan that Nancy had sent for her brother, they would have been waiting on him.

He rode past the telegraph office and tied his horse in front of Curd's Dry Goods Store. The telegraph office was two buildings north of there, so he walked along the boardwalk and went inside. The operator looked up but didn't recognize Sawyer—or if he did, he didn't say anything.

"Mr. Hoffman, you probably don't recognize me, but I'm Sawyer McCade. I wanted to ask you a few questions, if that's okay?"

The man looked hesitantly at a closed door to his left and then shifted his gaze back to Sawyer, then back to the door again. Sawyer got the hint and pulled his gun as he walked to the door. He pulled it open—the room was empty and when he opened the back door, no one was outside either.

"There's no one back there. They must have left. Did they cheat you out of the office and make you work for them in exchange for not losing your home?"

"They'll kill me if they find out I've talked to you," said the frightened man.

"You're safe. I won't let anyone know that we've spoken," said Sawyer.

"The bank stole my telegraph office because I was two days late on my bank payment. They delivered the foreclosure papers in person that Judge Elliot had signed over to the bank. I tried to pay them, but they said it was too late because the new deed had already been signed. I'm supposed to tell them about every message that I send and receive, but I didn't tell them anything about the one I sent for Nancy Lou."

"I knew that you had kept that quiet. Thank you for that. I wanted to let you know that changes are coming to town. You take care. I'll leave now so you don't get in trouble."

Sawyer got on his horse and rode to the building used as a courthouse. Before Sawyer left to go off to war, the building had been used as a library and housed two lawyer's offices. The original county building had burned, and the county was renting the current building. He went inside and registered as a candidate for county sheriff.

When he left the county election office, he rode to the sheriff's office and went inside to find the lawman leaned back in his chair, asleep.

"Hey!" said Sawyer. The startled man almost fell over backward.

"What do you want, coming in here like that? I ought to lock you up for disturbing the peace," said Sheriff Kiser while rubbing the sleep from his eyes.

"I suppose you could try to arrest me. I'm Sawyer McCade and I'm running against you for county sheriff."

"Boy, you're making a big mistake," said Sheriff Kiser. "The men who run this town ain't going to like that one bit."

"Since you're on their payroll, I'll leave it up to you to give them the bad news. You be sure and tell them that if they send their hired guns for me, I don't take prisoners."

"Now you listen here. I'm the law in this county and if you get out of line, I'll lock you up and take you before Judge Elliott."

Sawyer came toward the sitting man and hooked the leg of the chair with his foot. It tipped over, knocking the man to the floor. Sawyer stuck the barrel of his gun in the sheriff's mouth.

"Do I have your attention now?"

Wide-eyed with fear, the sheriff nodded his head the best he could with a gun against his mouth.

"You're not man enough to lock me up. And regarding Judge Elliott, you tell him that I'm coming to arrest him the day I'm elected sheriff. He'll share a cell with you, Hopson, and McMillan. Now I want to know who killed my folks and who killed Richard Straight?"

Sawyer pulled the gun away from the sheriff's mouth just enough so he could talk. "I don't know who did the killing at your folks' farm. They didn't share that information with me. But I'm fairly certain that Fargo was behind the murder of Richard. He either pulled the trigger or sent someone to do it."

Sawyer put his gun in its holster. He was disgusted with this man who was supposed to be protecting the town's citizens. He wanted to take his fist and beat the man until an inch of his life but held his temper and said, "There's going to be bloodshed before this is over. I suggest you stay clear of me because if I see you, I might mistake you for an ambusher and kill you."

He left the office, walked three doors down, and leaned against a porch post to wait. In a few moments, the sheriff came out of his office and hurried across the street to the bank.

Sawyer got on his horse and rode out of town, knowing that he had stirred up the hornets' nest and it was time to start exacting his revenge.

# Chapter Forty-Three

It was almost dark when he walked into the newspaper office in Iola. "Hello!" he called out. "Is anyone here?"

A man wearing a black apron came out of the back room wiping his dirty hands on a soiled rag. "What can I do for you, mister?"

"I'm Sawyer McCade and I filed as a candidate for Allen County Sheriff today over in Humboldt. I'm wanting to get some campaign flyers printed up. Is that something you can do for me?"

"It certainly is. Do you know how many you will need?"

"I'm afraid that the ones I put up in Humboldt will probably get taken down, but I can still put some up in other towns," said Sawyer. "I'm new at this campaign stuff. How many do you suggest?"

"I'm thinking five hundred should do the trick. I must admit, we don't have any representation from our current sheriff. If I were you, I'd hire some of the local boys to go around and put up the posters for you. That way, you can get them put up around the county faster."

"I don't know any local boys to hire. Do you have some in mind?"

"Yes, I do. I have three young men that do work for me delivering papers and running errands around town. I can get them to put these up in all the communities in the county."

"How much will everything cost me?"

"One hundred dollars should do it."

Sawyer counted out the money and handed it to the man. "I'll leave it up to you to hire those boys to put up the flyers. Make sure they get it done quickly, since the election is in two weeks."

"I'll take care of it. I'll also put an article in the paper on how you want to bring law and order back to Allen County, that is, if I can interview you."

"Sure, I can do that," said Sawyer.

"Did you know that the county seat is being moved from Humboldt to here in Iola?"

"No, I didn't know that. When is that happening?"

"It will be a few more weeks before the new court-house is finished, so most likely not until after the election."

"That's a new one for me also. I knew the old one burned down, but I assumed they would rebuild in Humboldt," said Sawyer.

"Have a seat while I go get my writing tablet."

Sawyer sat down and told the paper man about himself and how he wanted to bring law and order back to the good folks of Allen County.

He left Iola without visiting his sister. The less he was seen with her, the better it was for her. He was convinced that Hopson and McMillan had spies in the towns neighboring Humboldt. If he was in their shoes, he would want to know what he was up to.

On his way back to Humboldt, he stopped at farms along the road and introduced himself, asking folks for their vote. He remembered a few of the farmers from before he went off to war. He had discussions with a handful of people about some of their neighbors having their land stolen. The whole afternoon was spent campaigning, but he still had one more stop in Humboldt before he called it quits for the day. Tomorrow it would be a bad day to be seen in town. Hopson would have his hired guns waiting on him, so he would have to spoil their plans and not show up.

Sawyer dismounted in the alley behind the building used as the county courthouse. He entered through the back door and proceeded down a hallway until he came to a door with a sign reading, *Judge Elliott.*

He removed his gun from its holster, opened the door, and advanced into the room. The startled judge looked up, frightened by the gun pointed at him by a stranger in his doorway.

"What do you want? I won't go lightly on someone coming in here with a weapon pointed at me."

Sawyer closed the door, walked behind the desk, and lay the barrel of the gun on Judge Elliott's shoulder. "You're a crooked judge on Nathaniel Hopson's payroll, and I aim to put you in jail for your corruption."

"I don't know you, and I sure don't know what you're talking about. Now, get out of my office before I call for the sheriff."

Sawyer tapped the gun barrel on the man's shoulder. "That would be your greatest mistake, for two reasons. Number one, the sheriff won't come to your aid because he's scared of me. Number two, I'd cut your throat and leave you here in a pool of your own blood if you tried to call out for help. Now that I have your attention, I'm Sawyer McCade and I'm going to be the next sheriff. I'm taking down Hopson, McMillan, the crooked sheriff, and you. If you get in my way or come after me, I'll come back and deal with you. You can tell Hopson and McMillan that their reign of criminal activity is over in Allen County, and I'll be coming for them as soon as I'm elected sheriff."

Sawyer holstered his gun, went outside to his horse, and rode back out on the street. There, he dismounted and stood beside his horse to watch the front of the courthouse. The judge came out the front door and walked quickly down the street to the saloon and went inside.

Sawyer looked both ways down the street and decided to leave when three men exited the saloon and took up positions along the boardwalk in front of the saloon. Sawyer mounted up, pulled his gun, and turned down the street, riding past the three men. They moved to the edge of the overhang and stood side-by-side before they saw the gun in his hand. One of the hired gunmen grabbed the person beside him, said something, and stepped back.

Sawyer kept his eyes focused on the men until he was past them. He spurred his horse and took off north out of town. That little show of courage would give them something to think about. He turned east for a-ways and then south to Nancy Lou's house, planning to

sleep in the barn another night, although he figured it
wouldn't be until tomorrow that they started to look
for him.

# Chapter Forty-Four

During the night, it began to drizzle and eventually the rain got heavier. Sawyer woke up with his gun in his hand and listened to the sounds of the night. It was dead quiet and all he could hear was the rain tapping on the roof of the barn. He got up and poked his head out of the barn to look down the lane but didn't see anyone. What had woken him up? Had he been dreaming?

Two flashes of light blasted from the road, and he heard gunfire a half-second later. He waited and didn't give up his position. The shots hadn't been aimed at him since he hadn't heard any lead hit the barn. They had probably fired on the house with the thought that Nancy Lou would be asleep in her bedroom. He stayed hidden by the barn door, but after an hour they hadn't come up the lane to the house, so he lay back down and went to sleep.

Sawyer fed and watered the chickens, gathered the eggs, went into the house, and cooked himself breakfast. He went back outside, inspected the front of the house and found two bullet holes from the night before. One had hit the door, and the other one the wall.

He went back inside and cleaned up his dishes before he exited the back door and got the chickens to go back into their pen. He didn't want to leave them out, just in case a wild animal needed a good meal. Plus, if they were penned up, anyone who came calling would think that no one was home.

Next, he had something important to do, and it had to be carried out with precision planning and timing. He rode to his family home, where the workers in the field cut milo and put it in trailers. The foreman was nowhere to be seen, so Sawyer rode toward town until he found a good place to hide beside the road and wait for Lucas Killian to show up. Hopson's and his hired guns most likely weren't early risers since they like to spend their nights drinking; they probably stayed up late at night at the saloon and slept to midmorning.

It was hot already at ten in the morning, and for once there wasn't a breeze in Kansas. He waited until the sun was high overhead and finally saw his prey riding down the road toward the farm. Sawyer stepped out from his concealed spot and pointed his gun at the man. "Stop your horse and climb down, or I'll shoot you out of the saddle."

"Mister, this makes twice that you've pulled a gun on me. If you want to shoot, then do it, but I'm not getting off my horse."

Sawyer pulled the trigger and shot Lucas in his right shoulder, causing him to spin sideways in the saddle and fall off his horse. The frightened animal snorted and sidestepped to get away from the man on the ground.

Sawyer pulled the gun from Lucas's holster and stuck it in his belt. "Get on your feet. You've got some questions to answer, or I'll keep putting lead in you."

"You're crazy!" The man was holding his shoulder with blood seeping through his fingers and running down his arm. He was in pain and was making ugly faces each time the pain got worse. "I ain't going with you or answering any questions. If you know what's good for you, you'll get on your horse and leave the county," said Lucas, barely able to breathe from his pain.

"I'm going to give you that same advice after you answer my questions. Now are you going to walk, or do I drag you?"

"I'm hurt! I ain't going nowhere with you."

"Okay. have it your way." Sawyer removed the length of rope tied to Lucas's saddle and put it around the man's chest and arms. Lucas tried to fight back, but one hard whack to the head with the butt of Sawyer's pistol took care of that. Sawyer tied the rope to the saddle horn and led the horse toward the spot where his own was grazing. He rode his horse and led the horse that pulled the unconscious man for almost a quarter of a mile until they came to a creek.

Sawyer found a tall, sturdy tree, untied the end of the rope from the saddle, and threw it over a low-hanging limb. Then he tied it back to the saddle horn once more. He took some twine from his saddlebags, tied Lucas's hands with it, and then put one end of the rope that he threw over the limb around his neck.

He poured the water from Lucas's canteen over the unconscious man's head, making him wake up confused. Then Sawyer led the horse forward and tightened the rope around the frightened man's neck.

"You can scream and cuss all you want out here, but there is no one within two miles of us. I'll ask you questions and every time you refuse to answer me, your horse will take another step forward. Who do you work for?"

"You can kiss my nasty!"

The horse moved forward and tightened the rope.

"Wait, wait. I work for Hopson."

"I know you work for Hopson. I want to know who you get your orders from each day."

The horse took another step forward.

"Stop, I can't breathe!"

"Answer my question, and I'll have him take a step backward."

"I get my orders from Jamison Randall. He runs the saloon for Nathaniel."

"Is Jamison the one who gives the orders to scare the farmers so he can take their land?"

"Mister, you're going to get me killed."

"No, you're going to kill yourself right here, if you don't answer my questions. Is Jamison the enforcer who gives the orders to go after the farmers?"

"He's one of them. Jamison runs the saloon but takes his orders straight from Hopson and McMillan. They tell him what farms to go after and he makes the assignments."

"Who does Bucky answer to?" asked Sawyer.

"He and Fargo work for McMillan and only take orders from him."

"Who killed the man and woman out there where your workers are harvesting milo?"

"I don't know."

The horse took another step forward. The man began to kick his feet and gasp for air.

"Answer my question!" Sawyer made the horse back up.

Lucas took several deep breaths of air before speaking. "I don't know who did the killing. They don't involve all of us in the raids. The fewer who know, the better."

"Tell me who you think it was that killed them and Richard Straight."

"I don't know."

The horse took a step forward and he waited a few moments before guiding it back a step. "Guess who you think did it."

"My guess would be Bucky, Fargo, Kelly and Maxwell Wallingford, Lefty Branch, and Lesley Overstreet."

"Who's this Maxwell guy?" asked Sawyer.

"He's Hopson's personal bodyguard. No one goes against him."

"What does he look like?"

"He's a big feller and stays at the bank with Hopson."

"Where does Hopson live?"

"He lives upstairs in the saloon. The rest of his men live there also. McMillan lives on the second floor of the land office along with Bucky and Fargo. Kelly lives in a house east of the saloon with a woman named Stella."

"Who is Lefty Branch and what's his job?"

"Lefty and Lesley are two gunmen who work for Hopson. They live at the saloon, but you hardly ever see them in the main room. It's rumored that they spend most of their time at the old Thompson place owned by the bank."

Sawyer dropped the reins to Lucas's horse and said, "Thanks for the information. You're free to go, but I gotta warn you that if I ever see you again, I'll kill you. Be careful getting down and don't spook your horse."

Sawyer mounted his horse and rode toward the road. He could hear Lucas cursing him as he rode away. If you bullied people and lived by violence, it would catch up with you sooner or later. He didn't care what happened to Lucas, and rode away.

# Chapter Forty-Five

Sawyer rode into town from the south and took a secondary street to keep from being seen on Main Street. He tied his mount up behind Adam's Mercantile and went inside where he found Mr. Adams placing items in a sack for a customer.

Sawyer went up to the female customer and said, "Ma'am, I'm Sawyer McCade and I'm running for county sheriff. I'd be honored to have your vote."

She looked at him and smiled. "I knew your folks. They were such good, hard-working people. You have my vote, young man."

"Thank you so much. Would you be so kind as to keep it quiet that you saw me in town? I'm afraid my opponent will try to have me shot."

"Oh my, I sure hope not." She shivered and picked up her sack from the counter, and walked out of the store. Before she closed the door, she looked back at him. "Sawyer, I'll be praying for you."

"Thank you, I appreciate that."

"What in tarnation are you doing in town today?"

asked Mr. Adams. "They have armed men stationed all along the street, with orders to shoot you on sight. Hopson said he would give the man that killed you a hundred dollars."

"That's all I'm worth? That's disrespectful," said Sawyer, laughing.

"You have to admit that you stirred up a wasps' nest when you assaulted the sheriff and the judge. It's all over town that you had a talk with them and let them know what you intended to do."

"It was my intention to get their attention. They still don't know what they're up against. I'm going to find out who murdered my folks and my brother-in-law. Then I'm putting Hopson and McMillan out of business for good, along with the present sheriff and Judge Elliott."

"You should go out the back door and leave town before they start looking for you."

Sawyer went to the window and looked down the street. A couple of men stood by the leather shop and another man by the newspaper office. He thought about the boys that would be nailing up flyers around town, and it occurred to him that they might be putting themselves in harm's way. The only thing for him to do would be to eliminate as many of the hired guns as he could.

"Thanks, Alexander. I think I'll leave town."

He mounted up and followed the alley to the end of the block, then rode east. He tried to remember where the old Thompson place was. It had been a long time since he'd been there, but it finally came back to him. It was south a few miles, right on the river. He had fished there as a kid with his pa and friends.

He approached the house with caution and hollered out before he was in pistol range. "Hello in the house! Can I water my thirsty horse?"

The door opened and out walked a man most likely in his thirties. He was shirtless but wore a gun on his hip. "There's a stream west of those trees. You can use it to water your horse. Now get off my land."

"I'm sorry, I didn't mean you any harm. I'll go to the river." Sawyer turned his horse west toward the waterway.

"Not that way. You go back to the road and find your way to the water from there. Now get, before you make me mad."

Sawyer guided his horse back the way he had come, rode back to the road, and headed back toward town. When he had ridden out of the man's sight, he circled around and made his way to a stand of timber within throwing distance of the homestead. Leaving his horse tied in the trees, he proceeded on foot until he was close enough to see the movement through the windows. Since only one man had come outside, Sawyer assumed that he was alone.

The discipline of the Army had taught him patience, and he waited until he saw someone's shadow move across the window. Then he ran to the house and flattened himself against the roughly sawed planks. Staying as close to the wall as he could, he crept to the window and surveyed the kitchen. It happened to be empty. Only one dirty plate sat on the table. The man was alone.

With gun in hand, Sawyer backtracked along the side of the house until he came to the corner and peeked around to the backyard. He took one step to get around the corner when the back door opened. Sawyer stayed up against the wall and waited until the man stepped outside and was maybe five feet away from the door. Sawyer cocked the hammer on his gun and the man stopped in his tracks.

"Go ahead and try it," said Sawyer.

"Who are you, and what do you want?"

"I'm the nightmare you wake up to in the middle of the night, scared and drenched in sweat," said Sawyer. "Take your left hand and unbuckle that gun belt, and let it drop to the ground so we can talk."

"Mister, I'm going to kill you."

"Why did you have to say that and hurt my feelings? Lesley, that's no way to talk to an old friend. We both rode with Quantrill, but I guess you don't remember me. Now drop that gun belt, or I'll shoot you in the back."

Lesley did as he was told and then turned around. "You're the feller that wanted to water your horse."

"No, I lied. I wanted to see if you were here. I was a scout for Quantrill, and his men taught me some unique skills to convince a man to talk. So, I'm going to ask you a series of questions and every time you don't answer, I'm going to shoot your knees and then your elbows. If that doesn't loosen your tongue, then I'll cut off your fingers one by one. Then the great hired gun will be easy pickings for anyone that has a grudge against you or for anyone that wants to make a name for himself. That is, if you ever walk again after I'm finished with you."

"What do you want to know?"

"Who killed my folks and who gave the order?"

"I don't know your folks, and I ain't killed anyone since I've been here."

Sawyer shot him in his left kneecap, and the man fell to the ground, cursing. "I'm telling you the truth! I ain't been in on any of the raids or the killing of those farmers."

Sawyer shot him in his right arm. Lesley hollered out in pain. "You're crazy! I wasn't in on any of it!"

"Who rode up to Richard Straight's house and killed him with a shotgun?"

"Don't shoot me anymore, please. I'm hurting mighty bad. Lefty was with them that night, but I don't know who pulled the trigger. It was Lefty, Fargo, and Lucas."

"See, you could have saved yourself a lot of pain and grief if you had told me that to start with. Where's Lefty right now?"

"He's in town waiting on you. I was supposed to go but had the runs and didn't feel good."

Sawyer pointed his gun at the man and fired one more time, hitting him between the eyes. "That's for murdering the innocent people while you were a raider for Quantrill," he muttered. He reloaded his gun and went inside the house.

# Chapter Forty-Six

The aroma of food filled Sawyer's nostrils when he went inside the house to wait on Lefty's return. Whatever it was sure smelled good! He opened the oven door to find meat and potatoes simmering in a deep pan. This trip was turning out to be well worth the time. He didn't even have to cook supper.

He pulled the pan out and stuck a fork into the meat to check if it was done, which it was. After he filled a plate, he took it into the front room so he could eat and watch the trail up to the house.

He finished eating and put the rest of the food in a tin container with a lid so he could take it with him back to Nancy's farm. It was getting dark, so he went into the kitchen and lit a lamp to make Lefty think that Lesley was there fixing their supper.

It was dark when he heard horse hooves outside in the yard. The sound stopped and was followed by the squeak of a leather saddle as someone dismounted. Sawyer waited in the corner of the room near the door, with a gun in his hand. The door opened, and in stepped Lefty.

"Lesley, are you in here?"

Sawyer took aim and pulled the trigger. The bullet hit the man in the leg and the impact made him fall to the floor. Sawyer put the barrel of the gun against the man's head and said, "That's a warning shot. If you don't tell me what I want to know, I'll shoot you in the other leg and then both arms."

Lefty cursed and rolled over onto his back. He had a gun in his hand, and he fired at the same time that Sawyer fired a second shot. The bullet from Sawyer's gun hit Lefty in the neck, but the bullet from Lefty's gun hit Sawyer in his side. Sawyer shot Lefty twice more and then staggered to the kitchen where the lantern was located to see how bad he was hit.

He wet a rag in the water bucket and opened up his shirt. As he started to wipe the blood away, he saw that the lead ball had actually taken off some skin and made a furrow about a half inch deep and three inches long across his side. He held the rag to the wound to try to stop the bleeding until he could find something to bandage it with. In one cupboard he found a stack of dish towels. He went into the front room and removed the belt from Lefty's pants—it would work to hold the bandage in place for the time being.

When he finally had the wound bandaged, he went into the bedroom and lay on the bed to rest. No one would bother him tonight, and it would give his wound time to scab over. Tomorrow he'd need to leave early, before someone came to see what had happened to the two men.

Throughout the night, he had dreams about seeing dead people, plus one lingering dream that he'd had many times before. He lay in a ditch and men stood over him, ready to shoot him full of holes. He woke up drenched in sweat and heard himself call out to his mama.

It was a fever dream—the wound must have gotten infected. Sawyer got up and went into the kitchen, where he found a bottle of whiskey. Once he'd removed the bloody bandage, he lay down on his side on the bed and poured whiskey on the inflamed wound. He cried out in pain and grabbed hold of the quilt as the liquid made his skin burn. Tears filled his eyes and ran down his cheeks until the pain subsided enough that he could cover the wound with a clean bandage.

That next morning, he poured more whiskey to the infected flesh and then applied some healing salve that farmers used on their animals that he'd found in the kitchen. He walked out into the trees where he had left his horse the day before and mounted up to ride to Nancy's house. There he would rest and heal up for a couple of days before he continued on his quest to kill the men responsible for the murder of his folks and brother-in-law.

He rode slowly and put the palm of his hand on the wound so the pressure would keep it from bleeding. It wasn't the first time he had been shot, and it was not a life-threatening wound if he could keep the infection in check. He'd have to give it time to heal some before he could finish what he started.

As he rode up the lane to his sister's homestead, he could see that the rope he'd put across the trail had been disturbed. It lay on the ground like someone had untied it or cut it loose. It appeared that someone had come to the house yesterday or last night. He took his horse to the barn and looked at his belongings; nothing seemed disturbed.

Before he went inside the residence, he walked around to the front door and sure enough, the lock was destroyed, and the door was ajar. He drew his gun and walked inside. The rooms had been ransacked, although he had no idea if anything was missing. In the kitchen someone had made a terrible mess, scattering flour, meal, and other food items across the table and on the floor. He went to the bedrooms to find them both in disarray. It made him mad to see that his sister's undergarments had been tossed to the floor.

He shook his head at how predictable Hopson's hired men were. He'd figured they would come calling, and now that they thought she had abandoned the farm, Hopson would take papers to Judge Elliott to sign.

Sawyer changed out his dressing and applied more salve to the cut—it wasn't as red and irritated as before. He left the house as it was, surmising that whoever had taken the time to ransack the house would be back today. And he would be waiting on them in the barn.

The day passed so slowly and at one point he thought about riding into town to see what was going on but decided to wait another day. He had to go soon though, because he didn't want the judge to sign the papers on Nancy's farm. But today he would stay as still as possible and let his wound heal. Tomorrow he would reevaluate his plan and move forward.

Late afternoon, right before dark, he saw two men on horses ride into the lane that led to the house. They stopped and looked at the rope on the ground, then moved on to the house. One man dismounted. Sawyer didn't recognize him as one of the fast guns. He was probably a messenger, checking to see if Nancy had been back since they'd torn the house up. He went inside and came back out in a few minutes.

"There ain't been no one here since yesterday. I say we go back to the Star Saloon and have a drink."

"Do you think we ought to check the barn?" asked the other man.

"No, I can tell that there ain't been no one here. The rope is how we left it, and so is the house. Let's ride out. We'll check again tomorrow. The boss said they can't do anything with the place until next week."

Sawyer let the two men ride out of the yard. He thought about killing them, but they would be back tomorrow so he could do it then if necessary. Right now, he needed rest so his wound could heal.

# Chapter Forty-Seven

He rested in the barn for the next two days. On the morning of the third day, a buggy came down the lane. He walked from the barn and met the person driving the rig as it turned into the yard. "Hello, preacher. What brings you out here?" asked Sawyer.

"About dark yesterday, three boys came into town handing out campaign flyers with your name on them. The sheriff arrested them for disturbing the peace and put them in jail."

"I was afraid something might happen to them. It's sad when you can't let people elect their own county officials," said Sawyer.

"That ain't all. There are men posted along Main Street in anticipation of you coming to town."

"Do you know how late they stay out and how early they start?"

"Right after dark, they head for the saloon, and it's probably nine when they get started in the mornings."

"Thanks, I appreciate you riding out to tell me

about the boys. But there's not much I can do right now about them."

"If you think of something to get them out of jail, I'd appreciate it," said the preacher.

"I'll give it a lot of thought." They shook hands, then the preacher turned his buggy around and left.

Sawyer went to the barn and tightened the girth strap on his horse. He checked the loads in his guns and mounted up. He hated that he had to lie to the preacher, but it was for the man's own protection. He knew what to do.

The horse took his time and walked slowly toward town, giving the darkness time to overshadow the small city. Sawyer wanted to be in position close to the jail when Hopson's hired guns went inside the saloon to drink. It was unlikely anyone expected him to have the nerve to bust three boys out of jail, especially with all the hired guns in town.

He circled around town, came in from the riverside, and stopped at the livery stable to check on the boys' horses. He left his horse tied to the split-rail fence out back and pulled open one of the massive back doors. The hustler, who was just a boy himself, came out of the tack room with a lantern.

"Can I help you with something, mister?"

"Yeah, do you have the horses of the three boys that the sheriff arrested this morning?"

The boy looked around like he wanted to make sure no one saw him talking to Sawyer. "I have their horses in the corral and their gear right over there on the ground."

Sawyer pulled money from his pocket and counted out ten dollars. "Saddle their horses and leave them tied inside, then you disappear. This money is for your work and to keep your mouth shut. If anyone asks, they came after the horses when you were gone to get food, is that clear?"

"Yes sir, I'll get them saddled right now and skedaddle on out of here."

Sawyer left his horse and walked in the shadows, along alleys and in between buildings until he stood against the wall beside the jail. He peeked around the corner—there was hardly anyone on the boardwalk and only one wagon on the road, heading out of town. He pulled his hat down low to shield his face from anyone that might be watching him, then went to the door of the jail and went inside.

The place was empty except for the three young men housed in the cell. Sawyer put his finger to his mouth, gesturing for them to remain quiet. He pulled a key ring off a peg on the wall and unlocked the cell door. With a finger, he motioned for the boys to follow him, and they all exited through the back door.

They were careful not to be seen or make any unnecessary noise. When they were inside the stable, Sawyer handed each boy some extra money.

"Go south out of town and then you can circle to the north. I still want you to hand out flyers in the other communities and along your travels. If you need more, have the paper man print extras. Don't come back here under any circumstances until after the election."

"Thanks for getting us out of jail," said a tall, sandy-haired boy of about fifteen.

"You're welcome. Now get going."

Sawyer took his horse over to the back of the saloon and tied him out of sight. He went along the side of the

building and around the corner until he could look in
the front window. He made a mental note of where the
hired gunmen were sitting and what the bartender
looked like. This would help him when it came time for
action. He had learned that men were creatures of habit
and would usually sit at the same table or stand in the
same location whenever they went into a room.

About the time he was ready to leave and go back to
his sister's, he saw a man get up, say something to the
men around him and walk toward the back door.
Sawyer eased back along the side of the building and
watched the man walk down the alley to the street and
then turn east on the side street.

The shadows made it easy for him to stay hidden
where he could observe which house the man entered.
The man had to be Kelly, and he appeared to be on his
way to his girlfriend's house. Sawyer needed more
information about the surrounding area before he
attempted his abduction of Kelly. He would be one of
the easier targets to question since he stayed at Stella's
house. He would be by himself walking at night and
Sawyer could take him without any problems.

Hunger pangs hit Sawyer's stomach, so he decided
to take a chance and stop at the café for supper. He
might have to shoot his way out, but he'd done that
before and figured it could be a good opportunity to
campaign for sheriff.

The dining area had eight people eating their
evening meal. He kept quiet until he finished his food
since he didn't want to spend more time than necessary
out in the open. He left a half-dollar on the table and
went to the door where he could see out into the street.
It was still clear, and he didn't see any of the hired guns

waiting on him. He turned back so he could address the townspeople having their supper.

"Excuse me, I'd like everyone to know that I'm Sawyer McCade and I'm a candidate for county sheriff. My only campaign promise is to rid this town of the criminal element which has killed people and stolen farms and businesses."

One of the men put his fork in his plate and stood up. "I'll be the first to say that I'm voting for you, and I recommend the rest of you do the same." Everyone in the room started nodding their heads. "Thanks for your vote and your time, and please spread the word to your friends." He turned and left the café. It was time to ride to his sister's for the night.

# Chapter Forty-Eight

Raindrops hitting the roof of the barn and a loud boom of thunder woke Sawyer up at the break of day. He pushed the barn door open enough to see outside. The rain wasn't too heavy, so he dressed and saddled his horse. With his slicker on and his hat pulled low, he rode on into town to have breakfast. Again, he told the townspeople that were eating at the café that he would appreciate their vote. They seemed genuinely glad that someone was taking the initiative to run against Sheriff Kiser.

A man and woman at the table next to where he sat seemed pleased, and the woman said, "They stole our farm, and me and my husband had to move to town and find work to survive. That banker and land man are nothing but crooks that tell Sheriff Kiser what to do. Sawyer, you have our two votes."

Some of the others in the room begin to say out loud that he had their votes also. "Thank you all for your votes, and I won't let you down," said Sawyer.

His next stop was at the sheriff's office to collect his

flyers that they took off the boys yesterday. He didn't knock, just pulled his gun from its holster and pushed the door open. His sudden entrance startled the sheriff and his deputy, who had a cup of coffee in his hand.

"That's him! I want him arrested," said the sheriff to the deputy.

Sawyer pointed his gun at both men. "Not today. In fact, I should arrest you for stealing my campaign leaflets and for the false arrest of those three boys who work for me. Now hand over my flyers."

The deputy stood still with his cup half raised to his mouth.

"Go ahead and drink your coffee," said Sawyer. "I ain't got no quarrel with you just yet. It's your crooked boss that I have business with."

The sheriff pulled open a desk drawer and was reaching for something inside it, when the sound of metal against metal caused him to pause. Sawyer had pulled the hammer back on his gun in case the sheriff planned to pull a pistol from the drawer instead of his flyers. Sheriff Kiser kept his eyes locked on the barrel of Sawyer's cocked weapon as he pulled out the stack of flyers and placed them on his desk.

"You're a thief and a crook, and this is your second and last notice. Don't mess with me again. I'll not give you another warning," said Sawyer as he picked up the papers and backed to the door where he addressed the deputy. "When I win the election, you can keep your job if you're honest and still want to work. But if I find out you're crooked like he is, then I'll arrest you both."

Sawyer walked out of the sheriff's office. The rain seemed heavier now. As early as it was and with the rain coming down harder, the hired guns would stay inside, so he had time to go door-to-door along the street handing out flyers inside the shops. At the end of the street, he decided to avoid the side of the street where the bank, saloon, and McMillan Land Company were located.

He took his horse to the livery stable to get him out of the rain and then walked along the muddy street in the residential part of town. Plodding through the mud, he went to as many houses as possible, leaving flyers and talking to folks until he caught sight of a clock and realized it was almost ten o'clock in the morning. The hired guns were probably up and standing guard at the bank, saloon, and the land office. With the rain coming down, they had most likely taken up positions at the windows in those businesses where they could see who moved along the boardwalk and street.

He went back to the livery stable, mounted up, and rode down Main Street to show Hopson and McMillan that he was indeed in town. Would they come outside and stand in the rain to shoot at him?

He kept his pistol under his slicker so the powder would stay dry. No one came out of the saloon as he rode by, and that surprised him. Next, he rode to the bank and stopped his horse down the street a-ways so it couldn't be seen from inside the building.

He reached back and removed the .36 caliber Navy Colt where he kept it in a holster on his back. He opened the door with his head down enough to shield his face and let the water drip off his hat, then walked to the teller window. The teller greeted him. "Good morning, sir. May I help you with something?"

"I'd like to talk to the banker and see if he's interested in acquiring my farm."

"I'm sorry, but he's not in town for two more days. He's in Kansas City on business."

"Much obliged. I'll come back in two days," said Sawyer, and walked outside.

If he was in Kansas City, then that was where the big money was coming from. Sawyer wondered if McMillan had gone with the banker too. That must have been the reason none of their goons were out in the rain watching for him. It might be a good day to even the odds a little more. Kelly was probably full of information, and tonight would be his night.

There wasn't anything he could do right now to the Hopson's hired hands, so he decided to ride toward Iola and campaign along the way.

As he rode along the road that went to Iola, he stopped at every farm, asking them for their vote and visiting with the farmers about what their concerns were. He probably visited with maybe ten families while traveling the eight or so miles to Iola on his way to see Nancy Lou. Campaigning was a ruse to travel to see his sister, and it worked well. In Iola, his flyers were nailed up in numerous locations around town.

It was still too early in the day to visit with his sister, since he would leave town immediately after visiting with her. It was for her protection, and he had to keep her hidden as long as it took. He went to the café for his noon meal and talked to the patrons who were eating there. When he left, he stopped at each business along both sides of the street until it was around six and the businesses were closing their doors for the night, even though there was still an hour or more of daylight.

Lights were beginning to come on in a few houses along the path to the boarding house where his sister stayed. Since it was getting late and most folks were either cooking or eating, he didn't stop at residences and went on to the boarding house, where he was greeted at the door by the same woman he'd met when he helped move Nancy there. "Come on in. Nancy is in the kitchen."

"Thanks," said Sawyer. He made his way to the kitchen, where his sister held a small glass in her hand, cutting out biscuits from the dough flattened out on the table. She looked up and ran to him, giving him a hug and getting flour on his shirt.

"I'm so glad to see you!" She smiled with joy. "How have you been getting along without me, and what's been happening?"

"Come on, let's go somewhere and talk."

Sawyer filled her in on his campaign and the flyers the boys were putting up for him. He held back about getting shot and killing the two men. That would be for another conversation; he didn't want her to worry more than she already was.

When they were through talking, he left and headed back to Humboldt to have a conversation with Kelly. He hated to hold things back from his sister, but it was for the best. And he sure didn't want her to know what he planned to do to Kelly that night.

# Chapter Forty-Nine

It took longer to get back to Humboldt than he anticipated because he stayed too long with Nancy, and it was after dark when he arrived. Hopefully Kelly hadn't already gone to Stella's. He put his horse out of sight and hid between two buildings along the path that Kelley would take and waited for over an hour before giving up.

Disappointed that he would have to wait another night, he rode past the house where Stella lived and noticed lights in two of the rooms. He thought about looking inside but rode on home. Tomorrow night he would be in place at dusk, ready for his conversation with the hired gun.

When he arrived back at his sister's house, he decided not to go inside. It wouldn't be smart to light a lamp in case someone was watching. Instead he went to the barn as usual and unsaddled his horse in the dark before lying down to sleep.

The next morning, he didn't feel well and stayed in his bed longer than usual. He figured it was from getting shot. He finally got up and went to the house where he cleaned the wound and put more salve on it with a clean bandage.

He spent over an hour cleaning up the mess in the kitchen that the men had made when they'd ransacked the house. He only managed to clean the kitchen, but happily discovered some bacon that he could cook with the eggs he'd brought in.

After he'd eaten, he still felt tired and had no energy, so he walked back to the barn and went to sleep. The rain from the night before had cooled the air, and he was so comfortable, he didn't wake up until it was dusky dark. He'd slept most of his day away. But he still had time to make it into Humboldt before Kelly went to his girlfriend's house. He needed to have the conversation with Kelly today, since Hopson and McMillan would be back tomorrow, and the election was only a few days away now.

Sawyer waited on Kelly like a mountain lion after its prey. Past mentors had taught him to have patience when he needed to, and the waiting gave him time to think about other things. Hidden in the shadows for only twenty minutes this time, he heard the footsteps of someone walking toward his hiding spot. He pulled his gun and waited until the dark figure was even with where he stood. Two quick steps, and he had the gun barrel stuck against the man's side.

"Hello, Kelly. It's time we have a talk, or you can die here. Use your left hand to unbuckle that gun belt and let it drop."

"I don't know who you are, but I'm going to kill you for this," said the hired gunman as he followed Sawyer's instructions.

"Walk forward until we get to the next street, then turn right. If you cooperate, I'll let you live."

Sawyer picked up Kelly's gun belt and threw it over his shoulder, and Kelly followed the directions that Sawyer had given him. After they'd walked to the edge of town, Sawyer told him to continue to an old barn farther up the road. It was abandoned and far enough away that no one would hear them.

Once inside the barn, Sawyer tied Kelly's hands with a rope and then threw one end of the rope over a rafter to force the man to stand on his tiptoes. Sawyer pulled out his Arkansas toothpick and let Kelly get a good look at it before he cut him on his left bicep.

Kelly cried out in pain. "What do you want?"

"I want to know who the shooters were that killed the McCade family and set their house on fire. You were there and you're going to tell me what I want to know. I rode with Quantrill during the war, and I've been taught how to carve a man so that he'll talk. Now, who was along for the raid on the McCade farm?"

"I don't know. I wasn't there."

Sawyer sliced his right bicep again. Again, Kelly screamed and tried to get away from his cruel captor.

Sawyer put the knife against Kelly's thigh. "I can keep slicing you until you bleed to death. Who were the raiders at the farm?"

"It was Fargo, Bucky, Maxwell, and Jamison. Jamison and Fargo killed them."

"See, that wasn't so bad. And who killed Richard Straight?"

"That was me and Bucky. Bucky shot him with a double-barrel shotgun."

"So, you were there with him?"

"Yeah, I was there."

"Who gave the order to murder those people?"

"McMillan is the boss, and Nathaniel gets his orders from him."

"Tell me about the Star Saloon. Is the bartender Jamison?" asked Sawyer.

"No, he doesn't bar tend. Jamison wears a suit and thinks of himself as a fancy man. He has an office behind the bar where he works during the day. He comes out onto the floor every evening and meets with Hopson and McMillan."

"How many of their men are in the saloon each night?"

"Right now there are only five men at the saloon. We're missing a few hands and figure they took off for greener pastures."

"Was working for Hopson and McMillan worth dying for?" asked Sawyer.

"What?"

Sawyer moved with deadly, accurate speed as the knife blade sliced through the killer's throat. His lifeblood pulsated out onto the ground. The man was dead by the time Sawyer closed the barn door.

As he went to get his horse, a thought came to him. He took his horse to the livery stable and went down the boardwalk, glancing into the windows of the Star Saloon when he passed by. He wanted another mental picture of the inside, and to see where the five men that Kelly told him was there sat. With the information fresh in his mind, he walked to the hotel and rented a room.

# Chapter Fifty

Sawyer sat in a straight-backed chair by the window in his room, watching who came and went from the Star Saloon. A plan formed in his mind, but it would have to be carried out with total surprise and precision timing. There were pieces of his plan that he wasn't sure of yet, and he needed more time to calculate the risks as well as evaluate the different steps of his attack.

Not one person entered the Star Saloon the first hour after he started watching. If someone did come down the street to have a drink, they went to the other watering hole in town. Kelly must have been straight with him when he said that the only people in the Star Saloon were Hopson's and McMillan's men.

Both Hopson and McMillan should have come back to town earlier that day from the information the bank teller had told him two days earlier.

McMillan and his men could pose a tricky complication to his plan, since they didn't live at the saloon. Then there was Maxwell, Hopkin's bodyguard. Did he stay on the main floor and drink with the other men, or did he stay with his boss? Sawyer needed to check on that if he could. And he couldn't forget Jamison. In the evenings, did he socialize with the other men, or did he only converge with his bosses?

Sawyer definitely had gaps in his plan. That meant he would have to wait another day until he had more details, and hope that Hopson and McMillan had indeed come back today.

He got up from his chair, removed his guns, and positioned them for the night where they were in easy reach. He had just sat back down when he saw a man dressed in black come from the Star Saloon and stand on the boardwalk. He was soon joined by another man. They had to be Fargo and Bucky. McMillan came through the door next, and the three men walked north up the boardwalk. Sawyer watched them climb the stairs on the outside of the land office building and go inside. Lights were lit in the front room and farther back in the living quarters.

They hadn't taken the time to unlock the door when they went inside. He wondered if he could have a look up there tomorrow.

After thinking about his plan, he put his guns back on and walked by the Star Saloon for another look to see what was going on inside. No one was on the street at this time of night and the coal oil lamps that lit the street were getting dim as they ran out of fuel.

Sawyer peered in the window and saw Hopson's hired gunmen at two different tables. Sure enough, Maxwell, Jamison, and Hopson were at a table with a half-full whiskey bottle in front of them. At the other table sat two of the men that he'd seen at Nancy Lou's house his first day in town. He wasn't too worried about them—they were probably just gophers. After he looked in each of the big front windows, he went back to the hotel.

He lay in bed and thought about his friends in Texas. By now they should be in Tyler or east of there, gathering wild longhorns. Beautiful Abigale, the waitress he had met, she was a looker and he wished he had been able to stay longer and get to know her better. He thought about the upcoming election and hoped that he won so he could arrest Sheriff Kiser and Judge Elliott. They needed to pay for the crooked dealings they had imposed on the folks of Allen County.

He went to sleep but woke up shortly thereafter when something came to him in his sleep. Who was McMillan and Hopson's boss in Kansas City? How could he find out? Maybe he could question Nathaniel Hopson. He smiled in the darkness. That would be the highlight of his entire adventure. The man would break easily under pressure and give up the name of their contacts in Kansas City. McMillan could be the tough nut to crack, and his two men Fargo and Bucky would be his biggest adversaries. They were both hardened fighters and killers. He might have to adjust his plan just a little and think of a way to eliminate them.

It was time for sleep, and he would adjust his plan for those two tomorrow. Maybe he could think of something to get them away from the others, so the odds were not so stacked against him.

# Chapter Fifty-One

The next morning, Sawyer left his room long enough to eat breakfast in the café. The patrons recognized him as the man running for sheriff, and gave him words of encouragement and told him that they would vote for him. Their remarks made him feel good about his chances of getting elected. He stayed off the main street and walked to the church to have a conversation with the preacher.

Sawyer tapped on the front door of the parsonage, and again the preacher's wife opened the door.

"Come on in. He's in the kitchen. I'm leaving to meet some ladies at the church, so you can talk in private."

"Thank you, ma'am, it's good to see you again," said Sawyer as she walked past him. "Morning, preacher," said the young man at the door of the kitchen.

"Good morning, Sawyer. Help yourself to a cup of coffee."

"No thanks, I've had enough to float a log this morning. Did you know that Hopson and McMillan came back to town yesterday?"

"They came in on the afternoon stage and two other men got off right after them."

"Two other men? So they brought more firepower back?" asked Sawyer.

"I was told that the men who arrived on the stage were carpetbaggers and took rooms at the hotel," said Preacher Toliver. "It's rumored that they want to take over the farm equipment and seed business."

"We don't need more outsiders taking over anything in Allen County. Do you have any thoughts about the election in a few days?"

"From what I know, you should win it by a landslide. People here are tired of the banker and his hired guns in town. They're not sure if one man can clean up the mess, but they're willing to give you a chance."

Sawyer got up. "I guess we'll have to see what transpires over the next few days. I best be going, but I'll see you later."

Sawyer wondered about the two new men in town but surmised that they wouldn't be a hindrance to his plans just yet. His biggest obstacle would be timing his movements so that he could eliminate his adversaries.

It was early in the day, and things could get interesting, so he went back to the hotel and sat at his window to watch the street and boardwalk. Around eleven, Maxwell left the bank and went to the saloon. He only stayed inside a few minutes before he came out, followed by the two men he'd seen at one of the tables the night before. They took up positions on each side of the doors of the Star Saloon to watch the street.

Maxwell crossed the street and went into the sheriff's office. Shortly he came back out with Sheriff Kiser. Sawyer watched Maxwell stick his finger in the sheriff's face, and it seemed like he was awfully angry. Maxwell turned back across the street and went to the land office while Sheriff Kiser walked in the other direction.

Sawyer kept watching the land office until Maxwell finally came out, along with Fargo and Bucky. Bucky sat down on a bench in front of the land office while Fargo walked along the boardwalk with Maxwell. When they arrived at the bank, Maxwell went inside, and Fargo continued on until he was out of Sawyer's sight.

Something big must have been going on for Maxwell to get all of their men out. Then it hit him. Someone must have found Kelly hanging in the old barn on the edge of town. That was probably the reason Maxwell had gone to the sheriff's office.

Fargo walked along both sides of the street twice that morning. The undertaker rode out on his hearse and didn't come back until midafternoon.

They must have taken Kelly to the graveyard and buried him. Sawyer smiled. They'd be having a toast in honor of Kelly in the saloon tonight and would never see him coming.

He sat in his room the rest of the afternoon and watched the street. Right before dark, he took out his guns and checked the loads to make sure they were ready for action. As the town closed down for the night, Nathaniel Hopson and Maxwell walked toward the saloon together and went inside. Shortly after that, he saw McMillan, Bucky, and Fargo walk to the saloon as well.

Sawyer went downstairs and out onto the street. With the hired guns in the saloon, it would be safe for him to go eat his supper. The café crowd seemed talkative as they ate, and they asked him questions on how he intended to clean up the town.

Finally, he said, "I'll clean up our town by eliminating the trash." With that, he got up and went back to his room at the hotel.

# Chapter Fifty-Two

Sometime between nine and ten that night, McMillan and Bucky came out of the saloon and walked toward the land office. Sawyer sat still at his window and watched lights come on upstairs. After about ten minutes, both lights went out. He continued to watch the saloon for another ten minutes before he got up and went outside.

Sawyer stopped to look in the front window of the saloon. The two men sat at the same tables, with the exception of Fargo. Tonight he sat with Jamison, Maxwell, and Nathaniel.

Sawyer removed both of his guns from their holsters and cocked back the hammers. He stood outside the door, closed his eyes, and took a deep breath to quiet his nerves. Then he opened his eyes, pushed through the door, and fired both of his guns.

He shot Fargo in the head before he even knew what was happening. Blood and brain matter splattered on Maxwell's suit. Sawyer turned the gun and shot Maxwell and kept moving through the room and firing.

Jamison and Nathaniel toppled over in their chairs before they could even get a gun out to fire back. The two men at the other table were so surprised that one of them dropped his gun as he tried to pull it from his holster. The second man pulled his gun, shot too quickly and the bullet hit the back of the bar, shattering the mirror.

Sawyer turned toward the two men who were trying to shoot back and fired until both guns were empty. He had killed everyone in the saloon like a madman on a mission. The room was so full of powder smoke that it was hard to see, and his eyes watered as he stood looking at the damage he had done. He emptied both guns and put them back in their holsters before he pulled the Navy Colt out of his belt. Then he went from man to man to confirm they were dead. Six murderers lay dead in pools of their own blood. Sawyer lay the Navy Colt on the bar and reloaded his other two guns before he walked outside onto the boardwalk.

A light was on upstairs in the land office building, so he went in that direction. He looked over at the sheriff's office but it was still dark. With a gun in each hand, cocked and ready to shoot, he hid in the shadows at the bottom of the stairs. The door upstairs opened and out walked Bucky with McMillan right behind him holding a shotgun. Sawyer waited until he had a good line of fire and began to shoot at the two men. They both went tumbling down the stairs, landing on the boardwalk. Sawyer holstered his Colt Dragoons and again pulled the Navy Colt out. He walked down the middle of the street toward the sheriff's office.

Sheriff Kiser came out onto the porch and when he

271

saw Sawyer with a gun in his hand, he turned and ran down the street toward the livery stable.

Sawyer went back to the saloon where a few of the townsfolk had gathered inside and outside to see what the commotion was about. Sawyer went behind the bar, poured himself a mug of chalk and took a big swallow.

"Folks, the drinks are on the house tonight." No one seemed to want a drink at the time.

After finding a bag behind the bar, he went to Nathaniel Hopson's body and emptied out the contents of his pockets into the sack. He did that to each man before walking down the street where McMillan and Bucky lay dead. He took what valuables they had, including a set of keys. One of the keys fit the lock on the land office building so he secured it before leaving. He would need to search the building for documents pertaining to McMillan's criminal dealings.

After he left the land office, he walked back to the saloon where the undertaker was recruiting men to help carry out the bodies.

Sawyer reminded everyone to vote the following day. Then he walked to the hotel to rest. Sleep didn't come as he thought back to his parents and the agony they must have gone through at the farm that day. He also thought about his sister, having to see her husband get shot in the front of their house. Tomorrow or the next day, he would bring her back to her house where she belonged.

After that, he would pay a visit to the dishonorable Judge Elliott. Tonight's violence had been necessary to rid the town of murderers and crooks, but now he was going to make changes to his life and stop living as if he was at war. He had killed men, and that was a sin that required him to repent and become the man people in Allen County would vote into office as sheriff. He still couldn't sleep so he got up and went outside.

He walked back to the saloon to check on the progress of the undertaker. The men were almost finished and when they had the last body out, he shut and locked the door with one of the keys he had found on Jamison.

# Chapter Fifty-Three

Sawyer had breakfast early the next morning, then went to the bank and put a sign on the door: *Closed until tomorrow.* His next stop was at the land office, and then the courthouse, where people were lined up to vote. He went inside and opened the door to the judge's chambers, finding it empty. He walked down the hall to a big, open room and asked the ladies who worked there if they had seen the judge. They informed him that the judge had not come to work that morning.

He walked out of the courthouse confident that Sheriff Kiser had skipped town the night before. Now it seemed that Judge Elliott had also left town. Oh well.

Everyone was busy with the election, so Sawyer decided to saddle his horse and go after his sister to bring her home. Judge Elliott wasn't a physical threat to him, so he could wait until tomorrow or the next day to arrest the man for the crimes he had committed. For now, he would go get his sister.

Sawyer rode the eight miles to Iola with a sweet sense of bliss. All the bad guys that were responsible for the murders of his parents and brother-in-law were dead. He tied his horse to the hitch rail in front of the boarding house. Nancy Lou ran to him as he walked into the living room.

"We heard that you cleaned house in Humboldt last night!"

"Wow, news spreads fast around here," said Sawyer.

"Are you ready to take me home? Because I have my bags packed and my horse is saddled out back."

"Yep, and I have a business proposition for you. That is, if you want to listen."

"Of course I want to listen. You can tell me about it on the way home."

The next morning after breakfast, Sawyer and Nancy Lou rode into town and were met by cheering townsfolk. He had been elected sheriff by a landslide, and the judge from the adjoining county was on his way to swear him in.

Sawyer stood on the steps of the courthouse to make an announcement.

"I want to thank each and every one of you for your vote and support. I promise to uphold the law and never let outsiders come here and take over again. I'd also like to announce that my sister, Nancy Lou Straight, is going to open up the bank and operate it as bank president. She'll go through all the foreclosures that Hopson and his gang made and return the land back to its rightful owners. That includes Adams Mercantile, the telegraph office, and the newspaper office."

The townspeople cheered at the good news, and the new county sheriff looked over the crowd and smiled.

# A Look at

## Take No Prisoners (Sawyer McCade 2)

**Peace was the goal. Trouble had other plans.**

With the war behind him and the badge pinned to his chest, Sawyer McCade returns to Humboldt, Kansas, determined to clean up a town drowning in corruption. As the newly elected sheriff, he's ready to uphold the law and lay the past to rest. But peace is a hard thing to come by in the unforgiving frontier.

When a ruthless killer leads Sawyer into a deadly game orchestrated by a powerful crime boss, the trail turns darker than he ever imagined. Hunted by outlaws and accused of treason by the U.S. Army, Sawyer finds himself caught between justice and survival, fighting enemies on both sides of the badge.

As the stakes climb and old grudges come calling, Sawyer must choose: follow the law or deliver his own brand of justice.

Will he break free from the violence chasing him, or become the very thing he's sworn to destroy?

**AVAILABLE JUNE 2025**

# About the Author

Monty was born and raised in Southeastern Oklahoma in the small town of Sawyer, which is nested along the banks of the Kiamichi River. He's owned horses and cattle, riding the former and working the latter. Over the years, he formed a deep connection and respect for the Old West and the courageous folks who braved the wild frontier.

Monty is an avid reader and is particularly enthusiastic when it comes to Western authors and novels. His love of reading sparked his desire to write his first short story. He loves writing about real places and landmarks from the 1800s. In college, he wrote a ten-page paper about his grandmother, born in 1886, who married at fourteen and took in five orphaned nieces and nephews shortly thereafter. Monty's love for history and penchant for storytelling earned him an A+, and he hasn't looked back since.

Now retired, he loves to travel, fish, spend time with his four grandkids, and tell stories. He looks for inspiration for future books wherever he goes, and he is a member of the Western Writers of America Inc.

www.montygarnerauthor.com